The Crimson Pearl

By G. H. Teed

Illustrated by Val Reading and R. Kessell

First published in the Union Jack magazine,
2nd Series, No. 564, 1 August 1914.

Stillwoods Edition

Stillwoods.Blogspot.Ca

Catalogue Information:
Title: The Crimson Pearl
Author: G. H. Teed (1886-1938)
Illustrated by Val Reading and R. Kessell
First published anonymously in the Union Jack magazine, 2nd Series, No. 564, 1 August 1914.
This Edition by: Stillwoods, 2023
ISBN Canada: 978-1-998819-10-2
Blog: Stillwoods.Blogspot.Ca
Author Blog: http://ghteed.blogspot.com/
Storefront: http://www.lulu.com/spotlight/lulubook22

https://tinyurl.com/ve25d42s This link should go to a spreadsheet of all known Teed stories. The list is annotated with various information on the stories and my progress with recapturing the work. The library of Teed's stories increases almost weekly. Check at the Lulu.Com for the latest arrivals. Search for Teed. /drf

Keywords: Sexton Blake, Huxton Rymer, Yvonne Cartier, Solomon Islands

Contains Explicit Racial Language.

Cautionary Note: This series of books by Stillwoods are intended to make the stories of G. H. Teed, born in New Brunswick, Canada, available to collectors and researchers. The editor, or rather digitizer has not altered the original publication.

This story may contain language and racial terms that are not appropriate to today. I apologize for them; I know that the author was using his voice to excite and entertain an adventurous English audience. These works were published from 82 to 110 years ago. Most every work has characters of redeeming ethnicity within.

I hope you enjoy and share these stories; I have.

Doug Frizzle

Contains Explicit Racial Language.

A MAGNIFICENT 80,000 WORD NOVEL OF DETECTIVE WORK AND THRILLING ADVENTURE, INTRODUCING SEXTON BLAKE THE GREAT DETECTIVE—YVONNE, DR. HUXTON RYMER,
AND OTHER FAVOURITE CHARACTERS.

Special Holiday Issue

A Magnificent 80,000-word Novel of Detective Work and Thrilling Adventure, introducing the following Characters:—
SEXTON BLAKE - The Great Detective.
TINKER – Blake's Assistant.
PEDRO – The Bloodhound.
MDLLE. YVONNE – Adventuress.
DR. HUXTON RYMER, and
SAN – Chief of the Brotherhood of the Yellow Beetle.

New stories from **Stillwoods** published on **Lulu.Com**

Cassidy the Con. Man
A Corner in Vanilla
The Secret of the Strong Room
Mystery Island
The Treasure of the 'Isabella'
The Case of the Captive Emperor
The Gang Girl
Spanish Gold
Doomed Ships
Yellow Guile
Prisoner of the Harem
The Adventure of the Green Imps
The Mystery of Room 11

The

UNION JACK LIBRARY

SPECIAL HOLIDAY ISSUE

·THE· CRIMSON·PEARL

A Magnificent 80,000-word Novel of Detective Work and Thrilling Adventure, introducing the following Characters :—

SEXTON BLAKE - - The Great Detective
TINKER - - - Blake's Assistant.
PEDRO - - - The Bloodhound.
MDLLE. YVONNE - - Adventuress.
DR. HUXTON RYMER, and
SAN - Chief of the Brotherhood of the Yellow Beetle.

No. 564.   August 1st, 1914.   EVERY THURSDAY.

CAPTAIN PETER LAMPORT, president of the Eastern Pearl Fishing Company, with headquarters at Brisbane, Australia, bent forward and pressed one of several buttons on his desk. Almost immediately the single door of the office opened, and a young man entered.

"You wished to see me, sir?" asked.

The president nodded.

"Yes, Ferguson. Step close, please."

When the other had done so, Captain Lamport continued.

"How would you like a trip home, Ferguson? You have been here for five years now, I believe?"

The young man answered the latter remark first.

"Five and a half, sir. I should love a trip home, but —"

"A matter of expense, eh? Well, I think that can be managed, Ferguson, for I intend sending you to London on a special mission for the company. Wait!" he commanded, holding up his hand as the young man started to speak— "wait until I have finished.

"Firstly, Ferguson, let me tell you that the mission for which I have chosen you is of such an important nature that, were it at all possible, I would go to England myself. But, as you know, the Bill regarding Kanaka labour is coming on shortly in the Legislature, and my presence here is absolutely essential. At the same time, this mission to England must be undertaken, and on casting about for one whom I could trust implicitly, I decided on you."

"You are very good, sir."

"Now, what I am going to say, Ferguson, you must consider in the most confidential way. It bears on matters regarding the business which, so far, are known only to myself and one other —our manager at the pearling grounds at Thursday Island."

As he spoke, Captain Lamport unlocked a drawer in his desk, and, opening it, took out a small leather bag, which he laid carefully on the desk before him.

"This," he said quietly, "is the principal element in the matter. Step closer, Ferguson. There! what do you think of that?"

All the time he was talking he was undoing the strings which closed the bag, and now, as he drew the mouth open, there rolled out on to the spotless white blotting-pad a small object which made Ferguson bend forward with a sharp exclamation of utter amazement.

"That," resumed Captain Lamport, "is the only pearl of its kind in the world, Ferguson. You will see that it is not by any means the largest. In fact, we ourselves have found many larger. But take it up. Look closely at it. Do you see that crimson cloud which sweeps throughout it like an imprisoned flame? Do you note how, when you hold it full in the light, the flame seems to be alive?

"It is a freak of Nature, Ferguson. Some chance chemical occurrence has caused it, and the odds are almost anything against it ever happening again. As a pearl itself it is perfect, and worth a fortune. With the additional value given it by the crimson glow, it is almost priceless."

Ferguson laid the exquisite creation back on the blotter with a deep sigh.

"It is certainly magnificent, sir. It must be worth a tremendous lot."

"It is worth, in my estimation, close on two hundred thousand pounds, Ferguson. Many collectors would gladly pay that for it. Now I come to the reason for my sending for you, and for showing you the pearl. It was found by Hemingway, our manager at Thursday Island.

"During the opening of the oysters on deck he himself found it, and kept the find secret. He sent it on to me at once, and as soon as I cast my eyes on it I knew that here was a pearl which would be the cause of crimes innumerable were its existence known. There isn't a pearl diver at Thursday Island who wouldn't give his eye teeth to possess it.

"So far, Ferguson, that crimson flame which fills it represents nothing but a beautiful freak of Nature. I do not wish it to be the symbol of blood, but such it will be if its existence is known of. Therefore, it is my intention to get the pearl out of Australia as quickly as possible. That is why I sent for you."

"Then you mean, sir?"

"I mean that I am going to trust you with this pearl, Ferguson. The Kara Maru of the Japanese line sails for Hong Kong to-morrow. You will go by her, and transship at Hong Kong for England. On your arrival there you will hand the pearl to Lord Cambrey, our honorary president. I shall also give you a letter to hand to him as well.

"That for your general instructions; now for details. As I told you, Hemingway thinks that, so far, no one at Thursday Island is aware of the existence of the pearl; but this morning I had a long wire from him which may or, may not prove he is wrong. I will read it to you. Listen:"

The captain drew out a folded piece of paper, which he spread out and read:

"Two Chinese have disappeared from pearling gang. Went without wages. Discovered have travelled to Brisbane. May or may not know of pearl. Better be on guard. Will let you know any further developments."

"Now, that, Ferguson, may mean that Hemingway did not keep his discovery as secret as he thought. The telegram shows that he himself is beginning to have some doubts on that point. Of course, we don't know what may have impelled the two Chinamen to run away.

"They may be only seeking new fields, but if they do know of the pearl, and if that is the reason of their disappearance, it will be necessary for you to be on guard night and day.

"In my opinion, you had better hang this bag around your neck, and don't take it off until you reach England. Carry a revolver on you by day, and sleep with one beside you at night. The purser's safe would be no more protection against cunning and desperate Chinese thieves than so much cardboard.

"Now, I think that is all. Take the pearl. Attach it to your neck here. Then call on the cashier. He has instructions to give you sufficient funds for the trip. After that make your preparations without delay, and go aboard the Kara Maru to-night.

"She sails at six in the morning. By the way, I have had a cabin reserved for you, so you will have no trouble on that score. Have you any questions to ask before you go?"

"None occur to me," answered Ferguson slowly. "I think you have covered all the ground, sir. I am very grateful to you for your trust, Captain Lamport, and will guard the pearl night and day until I give it into Lord Cambrey's hands."

The captain nodded, and watched closely while the young man loosened his shirt at the neck, and attached the bag which held the pearl.

"That, in my opinion, is the best place to keep it," he said.

"I think so, too, sir. I'll wager no hand can touch me there when I am asleep without waking me. And when I am awake they won't get the chance."

"I trust you to carry it through safely, Ferguson. Remember, don't even think of its existence. Once that is known your life wouldn't be worth two straws. And now good-bye, and good luck to you.

"Cable me from Hong Kong, Colombo, Fort Said, and London. That will keep me posted on your movements. I might add that your successful carrying out of this mission, Ferguson, will be well rewarded."

A moment later the door closed after the young man as he made his way out to the cashier's desk, and so out of Captain Lamport's life for ever, though neither of them knew that then.

He found a substantial roll of notes awaiting him, together with two drafts for large amounts, one on Hong Kong and the other on London.

Captain Lamport proved no niggard in the matter of expense money, and Ferguson thought to himself that he was to travel more as the special representative of a wealthy government than as the late chief clerk of a pearl fishing firm.

He passed out of the offices with a springy step, his heart warm with anticipation. Five years and a half since he had left the old country. Five years and a half of arduous toil.

How well he remembered how, by chance, some Australian pamphlets had come into his hands, and how his soul had risen in revolt against the dingy, dusty surroundings of the London office.

You see, Ferguson had not yet reached the point where his shoulders had begun to stoop, where the pulsating ambition of youth had been hammered down into a constant fear that he might lose his place.

He had not arrived at the point where a man resigns himself to a lifelong bondage at the desk with the hope that he may be able to save a little something from time to time.

He was still full of red blood. He was still a rebel against the thraldom of the desk, and then, just when he was on the verge of surrendering without any further struggle, he had come across the Australian pamphlets.

He had read with glistening eyes of the vast stretches of country where a man's most necessary capital was his ability and desire to work. He had read of assisted passages to that country of opportunity, and then, at the very moment when he should have been laboriously copying the draft of a lease for the crusty old solicitor, he had decided to throw it all.

He had risen, picked up his hat, and walked out, never to return. That was how Billy Ferguson went to Australia. On his arrival there he found that a good many thousands of young men had read the same literature which he had read, and had been seized by the same decision which had grasped him. The consequence was that jobs were scarce.

At last, however, he had secured an under clerkship with the Eastern Pearl Fishing Company, and had thrown himself into his work with enthusiasm. His promotion was rapid.

Captain Lamport, a practical man himself, saw the merits of the young clerk's work, and steadily raised both his position and salary until Billy had been made chief clerk.

Now he was given a mission of the greatest importance —a mission that he entrusted with only because Captain Lamport couldn't undertake it himself.

If he carried it out successfully, the captain had hinted that his reward would be of a satisfactory nature.

Consequently, as Billy Ferguson strode along Brisbane's chief thoroughfare beneath the boiling sun, he vowed with all the determination of his nature that he would rest neither by night nor day until he had handed the crimson pearl to Lord Cambrey himself.

So he decided; but he little dreamed of the decision Fate had already made in the matter. Nor did he realise how soon Captain Lamport's forebodings were to prove true.

Before many suns had set, that vivid crimson flame locked within the priceless walls of the pearl were to signify not only fire, but blood, and the first life to go out under the implacable ruling was to be Billy Ferguson's.

There rolled out on to the spotless, white blotting-pad a small
object which made Ferguson bend forward with a sharp exclamation of utter amazement.

Bending over Ferguson was a man who turned sharply as Rymer entered. It was the silent Chinese passenger.

THE steamship Kara Maru came up the river, and berthed at the city dock sharp to the minute. That was six o'clock in the evening.

She was a boat of medium tonnage, and for some years past had been trading between Hong Kong, Brisbane, Sydney, and Melbourne, with a stop each way at Manila.

Lately she had been refitted and brought up to modern passenger conditions, and while there were many larger boats on the route, there were none more favoured by the travelling public than the Kara Maru.

Her captain and officers were Japanese; her crew and firemen, a mixture of Japs, Chinese, Whites, Cingalese, Malays, and even a few Melanesians. With such a conglomeration of humanity in her forecastle, it is not surprising that she was at times the scene of many terrible fights, out of which the Malays and Chinese usually emerged victorious.

On this particular voyage the white men amongst her crew could be counted on the fingers of one hand. There was a surly Scotsman in the engine-room —a man who knew more about the engines of the Kara Maru than did the dapper Jap engineer himself, but who would always drift about in a subordinate position owing to the demon drink.

There were three white men in the fo'c's'le —two of the number being nondescript Yankees who had been on the Kara Maru for two trips now, and the third a big, silent, grim-jawed man who had signed on at Sydney.

Where the latter had come from, none of his shipmates, not even the blood-thirstiest Malay, dared to ask. He had come aboard just previous to the departure of the Kara Maru from Sydney, and, in accordance with the custom in the fo'c's'le, he had at once been made the target for the coarse insults of the fo'c's'le bully —a big, murderous-looking Malay who had pirated and killed all over the East.

For some time the silent white man had ignored the shafts. A more expert student of physiognomy than the Malay would have read, not cowardice, but magnificent repression in the features of the white man.

But the Malay, incensed by the other's contemptuous silence and egged on by the fawning creatures who looked up to him, capped the insults by an epithet which no white man of spirit has ever been known to swallow.

While one might have counted ten very slowly, the white man sat immovable after the crowning insult had been hurled at him; then very leisurely he rose and strode across to where the Malay stood fingering the handle of a long knife which was thrust in his belt.

The white man paused before him and gazed into his eyes for a few moments, then what followed began so suddenly and ended so abruptly that not one of the onlookers could gain a clear idea of just what had happened.

They received a hazy impression of the silent, slow-moving white man suddenly turning into a bunch of steel springs; they saw the big Malay caught up like a child, whirled about in a dizzy circle and tossed like a bundle of rags beneath a bunk to lay there, limp and inert.

Following that the white man charged into them, and for ten minutes wielded mighty fists amongst them, until they fell this way and that. Then the cause of it all walked quietly back to where he had been sitting, and, resuming his position, calmly relighted his pipe.

Not a word had he spoken all the time, and not even a smile crossed his lips as he saw the baiters sneak out on deck. As for the Malay, he still lay where he had fallen, only a low moan from time to time revealing the fact that he still lived.

From that moment the white man was left in peace. Twice on the way up to Sydney he had awakened to find the blade of a knife suspended over his head, but the individuals who had been so murderously daring now lay helpless in their bunks, one with a broken arm, and the other with a dislocated shoulder.

Since the last attempt none had been daring enough to try it again, for the two nondescript Yankees, once bullied by the Malays, but now safe in the shadow of the newcomer, watched while he slept. So came the white man into the fo'c's'le of the Kara Maru this trip, and so was his position there established.

Though he kept silent as to his reasons for being there, and said nothing about his previous experience as a seaman, it was soon evident that he was not only the best man on board, but the best seaman as well.

And it is safe to say that, as the Japanese captain looked down from the bridge upon his new and ablest hand he never dreamed that he was regarding a man who was one of the most able and cultured men who had ever set Europe by the ears.

Yet such was the case, for the silent, grim-jawed man who toiled so laboriously as a common seaman on the Kara Maru was none other than Dr. Huxton Rymer, one-time brilliant surgeon, and now a down-on-his-luck criminal.

And how came he in such a place? None but himself would ever know the full history of the events leading from his last daring flight from justice to the present.

Since he had escaped from the grip of Sexton Blake in Devon, after his bold impersonation of Thomas Brail, the South American millionaire, his career had been varied. A ship which had picked him up in the Bristol Channel had carried him on to Cape Town.

From there he had worked up-country to Jo'burg, and after that had drifted across to Australia. Then had followed ups and downs until a little affair in Sydney had made it necessary for him to take a vacation.

Then it was he had sought the docks, and his reasons for going as a common seaman instead of travelling in the luxurious passenger accommodation was because of necessity, not choice.

His destination was Hong Kong, where he hoped to pick up something which would put him back on his feet, but, in accordance with his usual keenness, he kept his eyes and ears open for anything which might offer on the way. That is why his attention was caught that evening by something which the casual gaze would have missed.

It was just after dinner. Most of the through passengers who had come aboard at Sydney or Melbourne had gone ashore to have a look at Brisbane. Passengers for Brisbane had departed as well, and those who would join the ship at this port had not yet arrived.

A good many of the crew had been granted shore leave, and had tumbled over the side, intent on crowding all the pleasure they could inside the few hours at their disposal.

Forward and aft the loading gangs were toiling under brilliant arc lights, disposing of the huge bales of merchandise which the winches swung through the open hatches from the dock. A solitary Chinese seaman was on guard at the gangway which stretched out from amidships.

Rymer had not been one of those to get leave —a fact which did not disturb him, inasmuch as it was his fervent desire to see the last of

Australia as soon as possible. His work finished, he lighted his pipe, and leaned over the rail, thinking perhaps of the days not so long past when he had revelled in all the luxuries money could command.

He had been there for perhaps twenty minutes, when a rickety cab drove down the wharf and pulled up close to the gangway. Then a young man descended, and after paying the cabby called a man to look after his luggage.

"A young fellow for Manila or Hong Kong, I suppose," muttered Rymer, as he carelessly watched the new arrival. One trunk for the hold, a cabin trunk, and two handbags. Must be going for a long stay. Perhaps he is making for England. He must be keen to get away, since he comes so early. Hallo! What is their game?"

This last as his wandering gaze took in the two shadowy forms which were coming down the wharf.

"Chinks from the cut of them," he murmured, "What the deuce are they hanging in the shadow for? Why don't they come out and walk where they should? Now they have stopped. Now they are at it again.

"By thunder! I do believe that young fellow who has just arrived is the object of their attention. I wonder what their game is?"

He watched closely while the young man directed the removal of his trunks from the wharf to the ship, and as he passed up the gangway Rymer heard him say "Cabin 20." Then he disappeared from view, but no sooner had he done so than the two figures which had clung to the shadows sped across the wharf and drew up close to the Chinaman on duty at the gangway.

"Chinks all right," muttered Rymer again. "I wonder if they are friends of the man on duty there? That is Charlie Soo, and of all the yellow pirates in that cursed fo'c's'le he is the worst. Seems to be friendly enough with them, anyway. I think this little game may be worth watching."

He had been murmuring to himself as he watched the movements of the two Chinamen, but now he acted. After a careful look round to assure himself that he was unseen, he drew back from the side and dropped to his hands and knees in the scuppers.

Then he crept along in the shelter of the side until he came to the end of the gangway which projected inboard. Now the low murmur of voices reached him, and, as luck would have it, the scream of the winches stopped just then.

Sharp and clear there fell on his ears a full dozen words of Chinese before the winches roared again, and on hearing them Rymer drew back sharply and crept back to where he had been standing.

Those words were as follows:

"Cabin Twenty. We both go —Tang Wu as seaman, and I as passenger. We —"

That was all. But when he remembered his suspicion that the two Celestials had been trailing the young white man who had arrived a few minutes before, and when he recalled that the same young fellow had gone to Cabin 20, Rymer's shrewd mind began to get busy.

"It's as sure as anything that they are on his trail," he muttered, as he once more lounged over the side. "The question is —why? From his luggage and general appearance, I should judge that he is comfortably fixed, but I shouldn't take him for any fool millionaire blowing about loose. Besides, if those Chinks were only after his roll, they would have gone for him, before he came aboard.

"No; there is something definite behind their game. For instance, if their remarks are to be trusted, it looks as though they intended travelling on the ship with him —one as a passenger and one in the fo'c's'le. Now, they aren't planning as elaborately as all that without some strong motive. It is just possible that they may have a vendetta against him. But whatever it is, it is sufficient to cause them to stick close on his heels when he leaves Brisbane.

"Therefore, Rymer, my boy, it is something which may be worth investigating. If those Chinks have a game worth while, it is up to me to beat them at it. And now to find out just where cabin number twenty is, and to see what I can see."

Just then several of the crew returned from their leave on shore, and any deck spying which Rymer may have intended was out of the question, for then, at any rate.

He was able, by guarded questions, to find out from one of the Yankees where Cabin 20 was situated. He found it to be located on the starboard side, main deck, and a quiet journey from the bow to the stern put him in possession of the additional fact that it was just beneath one of the lifeboats, opposite the saloon entrance.

With this to go on with, Rymer returned to the fo'c's'le, He had two hours to himself before he should go on watch again, but instead of utilising the time for sleep, he busied himself at odd occupation.

First, he slipped out on to the deck, and managed to possess himself of a long coil of thin, but strong, rope. This he brought into the fo'c's'le with him, concealing it under his coat from the eyes of any officer who might be about.

That accomplished successfully, he next proceeded to measure off several lengths, until he had a piece perhaps thirty feet long. This he cut off from the main coil, and after concealing it beneath his bunk, took the balance of the coil back to the deck.

Then he returned to the fo'c's'le, and taking the piece from beneath his bunk began tying knots along it at intervals of about a foot. That done, he opened his coat and wrapped the whole piece snugly about his waist, buttoning up his coat again when he had finished.

His next procedure was to remove his boots, and since most of the crew went barefooted anyway, this caused no comment. Then he lay down in his bunk and calmly dropped off to sleep.

It was just midnight when the voice of the second officer boomed through the open door of the fo'c's'le, calling the watch, and, together with several others, Rymer tumbled up on deck.

The loading was now finished. The screaming winches were silent; the blazing arc lights extinguished; ship and dock wrapped in silence. The Kara Mara was ready to slip her moorings as soon as the pilot came aboard in the morning.

By the simple expedient of pushing himself to the front at the psychological moment Rymer got himself chosen for duty on the promenade deck.

Together with another seaman, a short, squat Malay, he made his way to his post, and, on arriving there, ordered his companion to move on aft.

The latter made no difficulty about doing so. Doubtless, his fear of the big white man settled any objections he may have had. At any rate, he walked on obediently until he came opposite the smoking saloon and there he remained.

After a cautious look round near the entrance to the main saloon Rymer also made his way to the after part of the promenade deck, and stood in the shadow close to the Malay.

Through the ports he could see several of the male passengers gathered about the saloon —some drinking and talking, others gaming, and still others reading or looking on.

Taken together they were a cosmopolitan gathering. There were sheep and cattle men from the South and New Zealand; prosperous planters from Fiji; sugar planters from Northern Queensland; pearling men from Thursday Island; wealthy Chinese returning to China; inscrutable Japs whose purpose in being so far south may have been most anything; a sprinkling of the inevitable British globe trotter; and a few who were frankly adventurers.

With the eye of an expert Rymer sized them up and classified them. And it was not hard for him to pick out the man for whom he was looking. He saw him sitting alone over in one corner sipping a whisky-and-soda and languidly watching a game of poker which was proceeding at the table next to him. For the first time Rymer got a square look at his face, and he turned away he muttered:

That young fellow has never been mixed up in any Chink gambling joint; he is not that kind. So those two yellow Chinks can't be after any roll he picked up in one. This thing begins to get interesting. He is the type of conscientious young Englishman trusted by his employer. At any rate, he hasn't turned in yet, and if that slant-eyed mate will keep out of the way I may be able to find out something."

He sauntered back towards the forward part of the promenade deck and took up his station against the rail just beneath the overhanging boat. Twice the mate passed within the space of thirty minutes, but, when the smoking-room lights were extinguished and the passengers had dispersed, Rymer was left comparatively alone.

Suddenly directly beneath him a light flashed out and made a wide patch on the water beneath. Leaning still farther over the rail Rymer could see that it came from the cabin below, and that cabin he knew was number twenty.

He waited another ten minutes, and afterwards congratulated himself that he had done so for, at the end of that time, the mate came round again. Then he passed, and no sooner had he disappeared aft than Rymer got busy. He knew he was about to take a big risk, but he had decided, if he were caught, to drop into the water and get away if he could.

First he opened his coat and unwound the rope from his waist. One end of this he tied firmly to the lifeboat overhead, and the other end dangled over the side. Then, with a final look round, he drew himself up on the rail, grasped the rope with both hands, and swung himself over.

Gripping the rope by the knots he had tied in it, and fending himself off from the side with his bare feet he began to descend. Just beneath him he could see the gleam of light in the porthole of cabin number twenty, and a shadow which flitted across from time to time told him the occupant was preparing to retire.

Still he kept on in his descent. At last his toes touched the grooved brass rim which overhung the port. There he halted, his feet slipping one to the right and the other to the left of the port. Then he lowered himself still further, lying back against the rope as he did so.

Another six inches and he found himself gazing into the interior of the cabin. He had made no mistake in either the number of the cabin or the young man he had seen in the smoking saloon, for the man inside, who was preparing to turn in, was the same.

As Rymer looked in he was sitting on the edge of his bunk in his pyjamas. In his hand he held his watch, which he was winding. This done he stuffed it under his pillow and rose. Then Rymer saw him go through a curious pantomime.

First he walked to the door and shot the bolt, then he took from a pocket in his trousers, which hung behind the door, a revolver of heavy calibre. This he laid on the bunk.

Sitting down again he unbuttoned the top button of his jacket, and, thrusting his hand inside, drew out a small black bag, which was tied about his neck. With deft fingers he undid the mouth of it and turned it upside down.

Something dropped into his hands, but what it was Rymer could not see. A moment later, however, the young fellow on the edge of the bunk held up an object between his thumb and first finger. Then, as the rays from the light overhead caught it, the man who watched from outside gave an involuntary gasp of utter stupefaction.

To him it seemed as though the man in the cabin was holding a sphere of living flame in his hands, so lifelike did its fire appear beneath the whiter light above. In a flash he grasped what it meant, and with the knowledge there came into Rymer's heart an unholy desire to possess it.

Now he knew why the young fellow had been so persistently trailed by the two Celestials. Now he knew why they were arranging to travel by the Kara Maru.

And now he knew that he, himself, would not rest until he had beaten them both in their race for that sphere of flame, be the cost what it might.

He made his way back to the deck strangely shaken by his discovery. He found that his absence had passed unmarked, and when the next watch was called he welcomed the release from duty.

He wished first to rid himself of the rope, then to seek his bed and pit his brains against those cunning Oriental minds which he knew were already at work on the Kara Maru.

The young fellow on the edge of the bunk held up an object between his thumb and first finger. Then——

As the rays from the light overhead caught it,
the man who watched from outside gave an
involuntary gasp of utter stupefaction.

III.

THE Kara Maru dropped down the river with the dawn next morning. She made the bay beyond without incident, and after dropping the pilot set her nose past Moreton Island and headed towards the Great Barrier Reef on her long voyage to Hong-Kong.

Neither in the passenger quarters nor in the fo'c's'le were there any signs during the next few days that an undercurrent of intrigue was aboard.

Amongst the passengers who had joined the ship at Brisbane was a quiet-mannered Chinaman. He had come aboard late at night, and, so far, had kept strictly to himself.

No comment was caused by another addition to the crew, for such was a common occurrence, and certainly no casual observer would have placed any connection between the new Chinese member of the fo'c's'le and the quiet Celestial passenger.

Rymer, however, took careful note of the new-comer in the fo'c's'le, and watched closely to see if he held any communication with the man who travelled as a passenger. He felt certain that the flaming pearl he had seen was what they were after, and he felt equally as certain that they would make an attempt to gain possession of it before the Kara Maru reached Manila.

Consequently, he did not relax his espionage a single moment. He built many theories as to what would be the probable course of procedure of the Celestials. The one who travelled as a passenger would, he thought, be the one to make the theft when occasion offered.

But what his exact plan of action would be Rymer couldn't tell. He knew those shrewd brains were capable of the most subtle schemes, and strained his own ingenuity to guard against any move they might make.

The Chinaman in the passenger quarters might enter cabin twenty at night, and, after robbing the occupant of the pearl, pass it on to his confederate in the fo'c's'le.

Again, either of them might assault Ferguson (Rymer had discovered that to be the young fellow's name) while he loitered on deck at night. If the latter were done he knew Ferguson would have mighty short shrift, and that he would be forced over the side to make food for the fishes.

18

Therefore, Rymer watched Ferguson, too, and little did that young man dream of the attention he was receiving. So far Rymer felt that his own intentions were unsuspected by the two Celestials, and, as a matter of fact, this was so.

In this fashion did the Kara Maru steam along the "Barrier," with the plotters which she carried marking time. Then something happened which entirely spoiled whatever plans may have been laid by the Celestials and brought things to a crisis for Rymer.

For two days now the sky had been murky. From the north-west a steady hot wind had been blowing which seemed to slip over the oily face of the sea as though the latter were greased.

The atmosphere which hung over all was depressing, and though the breeze blew steadily there was no relief in it from the heaviness of Nature. Men who knew those waters well glanced anxiously at the sky from time to time and frowned at the treacherous Great Barrier Reef which lay so close to them.

The officers watched the falling glass closely, and the captain strained every effort to get through Torres Strait before the climax should come. It was on the fifth night out of Brisbane that the crash came.

Eight bells had just gone. Most of the passengers had turned in, though a few still remained in the smoking saloon. Since sunset the wind had dropped entirely, and the air seemed like a gigantic blanket weighing down the face of the sea.

Even the Malays, accustomed as they were to such conditions, lay gasping for breath, whilst the Chinese and Cingalese squatted just outside the fo'c's'le watching the murky sky with inscrutable eyes.

Then a low moaning sound broke upon their ears. At first it might have been taken for a distant choir sending forth its united powers over the black face of the sea.

But as it grew louder in volume it was more as if the host of Nature were marshalled overhead tearing along in their gigantic chariots to the blare of the trumpets of the advance guard.

Just when the strange, uncanny noise had swelled to a great roar which filled the ship from end to end the voice of the captain sounded from the bridge.

Like men awaking from a dream the crew sprang to their feet and leaped to obey the orders which he screamed. But they might as well have battled against the sea itself for, at that moment, the ship heeled over as though the "Barrier" had risen upwards.

Over, over she went under a terrific pressure, then back she came, and hard on this the shrieking tempest broke. Words fail to describe what followed.

Everything which was not tied to the deck went by the board under the first lash of the hurricane; two Chinamen and a Malay were lifted up bodily and hurled over the side into the sea; huge ventilators went down like ninepins, and the ship herself bent under the awful pressure with sickening surrender.

Then, as though she had gathered strength for further resistance, she lifted herself and caught up by the tempest shot ahead through the tossing white-lipped cauldron which such a short time before had been a placid sea of ink.

No engines made of iron, no seaman afloat, could guide a ship through that awful cataclysm of Nature. Whither the Kara Maru was driving none knew. All her captain could do was to keep her helm hard down and wait for the blast to spend itself.

But as the dark hours of the night passed it seemed to gather in strength rather than to weaken, and when even above the roar of the gale another and more sinister noise arose did the faces of the bravest blanch. Not one amongst them but knew the meaning of that never-to-be-forgotten noise —the rolling of the surf on a coral reef.

Dawn came slowly and reluctantly, lighting up the boiling cauldron through which they were driving. Away to port showed a high line of white foam where lay the reef. Fate had sent them past it, and for the time being they had only the gale to combat.

All that day officers and men laboured incessantly to keep the Kara Maru on her course, for the chart showed many reefs and islands ahead, and well they knew what that meant did they drive in amongst them.

The passengers clung to the saloon, only the hardiest venturing out to brave the tempest-swept decks. Night closed down again with the scene unaltered. They were still driving ahead in the teeth of the gale, which now was shrieking forth its anger from the south-west.

It was just past ten o'clock when the propeller went, and hard on that again came the roar of surf. The orders went out for boats, though in his heart each man believed the order was hopeless.

To launch a boat in that sea was madness. It could not live a moment. Yet, still true to their training, the crew leaped to obey —all but one. That one was the big, silent white man who ruled supreme in the fo'c's'le.

As the others hurried to the falls he slipped along the main deck until he came to the entrance to the cabins. Passing through he turned into a passage leading to the left, and kept on until he came to a door numbered twenty.

For a moment he stood listening, then turning the handle opened the door. As he pushed it inwards and stood on the threshold, a startling sight met his eyes. Lying on the bunk was the man whom he had come to seek —Ferguson.

But he was not alone, and in his first brief glance Rymer saw that he was already where shipwrecks and intrigue mattered not. Bending over him was a man who turned sharply as Rymer entered.

It was the silent Chinese passenger, and as he saw the tall figure of the white man at the door he snarled with rage. In his hand he held a Malay kris, and the crimson stain on the throat of the prostrate Ferguson told only too plainly how it had been used. Already the crimson flame of the pearl symbolised blood.

Rymer stood watching the Chinaman warily. Inch by inch he moved forwards until he was clear of the door. This he kicked to with his heel, and as it slammed behind him he backed up against it. Not till then did the Celestial speak.

"What you want?" he demanded tensely.

For the first time since he had come aboard the Kara Maru, Rymer smiled.

"I might ask what you want?" he answered curtly. "What means this?"

"Who are you to ask?"

"Never mind. Answer me. This man has been murdered. I find you bending over him with a knife in your hand, and the blade is red. Is it because you wish for what hangs about his neck?"

So softly did Rymer utter the last words that, for a moment, they failed to penetrate the Celestial's hearing. But when they did he bent almost double with fury, and without the slightest warning hurled himself upon Rymer, his knife raised to strike.

Rymer stood motionless until he could almost feel the breath of the other upon him, then his muscles suddenly grew taut, and he turned into a bundle of steel springs as he had in the fo'c's'le on his arrival on board the Kara Maru.

His left hand shot out and grasped the right wrist of the other in a grasp of iron. His own right hand plunged for the throat of the Celestial, and his fingers closed upon it.

Then he braced his legs against the shock of the impact, it came a second later, and together they went crashing back against the door of the cabin. Straining, twisting, struggling, they went lurching about the cabin, forgetful now of that sinister scarlet stained figure which lay in the bunk.

As though from a great distance the shrieking of the tempest reached them, and overhead could be heard the scurrying of feet as passengers and crew rushed the boats.

But not a single boat was destined to leave the Kara Maru that night. No sooner did one strike the water than it was hurled against the side, and crushed like an eggshell by the mountainous waves. Boat after boat met the same fate, until only two were left, and these the captain held for eventualities.

All hands now feverishly sought life preservers in a last hope to be ready for the worst when it came, and it seemed as though it must come soon. Louder and louder could be heard the beating of surf on reef as the Kara Maru drove helplessly before the gale, her rudder a frail reed to lean upon, her propeller at the bottom of the sea.

Such were the conditions as those two men struggled madly in the cabin below, each oblivious to everything but his one mad desire to overcome the other, and secure for his own that sphere of imprisoned flame.

Though much the larger in stature and possessed of greater strength than his opponent, Rymer was handicapped by the fact that the Celestial still gripped the knife between his fingers.

All the white man's brute strength had not yet succeeded in forcing those yellow claws to loosen. And well Rymer knew how expertly the knife would be wielded once the other got his arm free.

They were now by the door, again fighting for the mastery. In a gigantic effort which caused his own muscles to ache, Rymer got his man against the door, then crouching slightly he concentrated all his strength on a tremendous heave which forced the Chinaman's right hand up, up, up, until the blade of the knife pointed backwards towards the door.

Half closing his lids in order to hide his intent from the gaze of the other, Rymer now lurched backwards, pulling the Celestial with him. Then suddenly putting forth every atom of strength and weight he heaved forward again, driving the Chinaman's hand back over his shoulder, and sending his head crashing against the door.

A sickening thud followed, and though the Celestial kept his senses, his eyes gleamed with the first look of fear as he found the thrust had sent the point of the blade so deeply into the soft wood of the door that he could not withdraw it again. Seeing the success of his strategy, Rymer redoubled his efforts, and concentrated all his strength on the other's throat.

Just then both combatants were hurled backwards to the floor as a terrific crash sounded, and the Kara Maru stopped with a shiver which shook her from stem to stern. The fear-laden cries overhead told Rymer only too plainly what had happened. What had been dreaded had come. The Kara Maru had gone on a reef.

Even in the teeth of death by drowning, Rymer turned to renew the struggle, but a single glance told him it was not to be necessary. The Celestial lay unconscious where he had fallen, a great gash in his forehead.

Quickly Rymer scrambled to his feet, and hurried across to the bunk where the body of the dead Ferguson lay. Feverishly his fingers sought the bag which he knew had been suspended from the young fellow's neck, and a quiver of joy went through him as he felt it.

Jerking it out he tore it bodily from the string which held it; then opening the mouth of the bag he let the pearl drop out on to his palm. One long look of utter fascination he threw at the glorious gem, one expert touch he gave it; then, thrusting it back into the bag, he stuffed it into his inside pocket.

He gave a last look at the prostrate figure of the Chinaman, then made for the door; now he could plainly hear the shrieks of the people on deck, and though he knew the Kara Maru was doomed and that he stood every chance of being caught like a rat in a trap, he turned back again as a fresh idea occurred.

With deft fingers he went through the pockets of both Ferguson and the Celestial, stuffing the contents in his own. That done he jerked down the lifebelt which lay in the rack overhead, and buckled it on.

Now he again made for the door, and just as he reached it he felt the ship rise up and drop with another fearful crash. Complete and utter darkness followed as the lights went out, and to the accompaniment of shrieks, curses and groans, smashing timbers and rushing water, Rymer fought and scrambled along until he finally emerged on deck.

There a terrible sight met his eyes. That the ship was done for, there was now no question. Crew and passengers fought with equal ferocity for the two remaining boats. Ahead stretched the white line of the breakers; behind was the blackness of the storm-swept sea. And all the time the poor stricken ship pounded her life out on the jagged reefs.

Rymer was seaman enough to realise that no boat could live in that boiling death for a moment, and he was cool enough to see that to remain on the ship was to meet death very quickly.

Two hours before he had not cared very much whether the Kara Maru went to the bottom or not, but now, since he had felt the touch of that flaming pearl, he was a different man. He wanted desperately to live and, if it were possible to clutch his life out of what seemed certain death he intended to do so.

Swiftly his eyes swept the line of white ahead. Far to the right he saw a break in the line, which told him there might be a channel there. If he could reach it and fend himself off from the jagged reef until he got through, he would at least be in calmer water on the other side.

A keen, searching gaze in every direction told him no other chance offered. This was his only hope of safety, and slender though it was he decided to take it.

He pushed his way to the side and, raising himself up, dropped over. A moment later he was being swept along at a terrific pace towards the break in the line of foam.

End of Prologue.

Rymer watched closely while the two figures drew up close to the China-man on duty at the gangway.

The Story Begins

IF either travel or study has led you to investigate the myriad isles of the South Pacific, your mental or actual wanderings will have brought to your ken those densely-clad, coral-reefed cones known as the Solomon Islands. Lying as they do just south of the equator and in the line of the monsoon, the climate is unhealthy for the white man, and in fact even were it not unhealthy on that score it would still be in another, for the islands are one of the last strongholds of pure cannibalism.

Within the shadow of the magisterial and trading stations little of this practice is seen, but back in the bush, where neither traders or government expeditions penetrate, it still flourishes unabated.

The islands themselves are ideally formed for the lazy savage tribes which inhabit them. A bare half dozen reach any size, but hundreds of smaller ones go to make up the archipelago. And in no corner of the globe does such riotous beauty prevail.

Island after island stretches before the eye —each one a vivid emerald set in a boundless ocean of sapphire. The intense azure of the sky but deepens the soft blue of the sea, and only where the surf rolls gently against the reefs of living coral can one see the white foam which lies locked in all water.

To approach one of the islands is to revel in a riotous array of colour which defies description. As the barrier reef is reached one can glance down into the limpid depths and see a garden of living coral which rivals the most exquisite creations of man.

Every colour of the rainbow is there —blue and pink, green and red, orange and purple, and browns of every shade, and shooting amongst the fronds with the swiftness of light itself are myriads of tiny vividly coloured fishes.

Then sloping upwards this submarine garden merges into the atoll through which stretches the passage into the lagoon beyond —a passage reminding one of a lost canal built through the heart of a dense tropical forest, or a lost water lane in the delta of an equatorial river.

Rising on every side one sees the graceful coconut palms, whose bursting branches trace their delicate pattern against the blue dome overhead, whilst banked against their slanting stems is the dense and almost impenetrable undergrowth which spreads over the tropics with incredible swiftness.

Orchids there are in profusion, their great coloured blossoms hanging heavily in their dark humid retreats; pepper and areca nuts; cinchona and ferns; all massed together in a tangle of tree and bush and plant which presents the intricacies of a Chinese puzzle.

And the birds! Glorious birds of paradise —some coal black, some mildly white and yellow, but most a blend of flashing colour. Parrakeets abound, sending forth their shrill cries in defiance of all; parrots and cockatoos and, farther in the depths of the forest, hornbills.

Altogether a paradise of man, yet given up to the uncivilised Melanesian, whose greatest desire in life is the hunting of his fellow man.

Such an island is the small and almost unknown island of Rubilinga, where lives the famous and feared Rubilinga tribe, and is situated a single trading station.

In charge of this solitary outpost of the white man was a rugged Australian, to whom the islands have been home for many years.

He it was who met the tribes as they brought in their offerings of pearl-shell and tortoise-shell, and gave them in exchange the cheap knives or axes which they value so highly, the rolls of vividly coloured cloth, the strings of cheap beads, or that universal article of exchange trade, tobacco.

He it was who was still there several weeks before, when the unruffled serenity of Rubilinga was broken by the arrival of another white man. Where the latter had come from, Johnson, the Australian trader, never knew. Nor did he ask. Such questions are deemed in bad taste in that part of the world.

He only knew that the new arrival was an Englishman of forbidding mien, and that within half an hour of his arrival, he had proclaimed his intention of making an indefinite stay in Rubilinga.

Now, the trading station of Rubilinga is composed of, firstly, a long, low-lying, wooden shack, which is dignified by the name of "store." There the bartering with the natives took place. Adjoining this was a smaller shack, heavily thatched, where Johnson lived with his native wife and half-caste children.

Farther back, in a grove of coconut palms, were the huts of his native labourers, for the Australian had many acres of coconuts which produced much copra. Around the main building ran a rough stockade as a measure of safety against the natives, should they evince a sudden desire for the white man's head.

This array of buildings was close to the fringing reef of the lagoon, and was set in the heart of beauty hard to surpass. And this it was which composed the main village. Back in the depths of the forest, or farther along the shore of the lagoon, lay other scattered shacks, where the Rubilinga tribes lived or made their headquarters.

Impelled by a natural dislike of the new arrival, Johnson the trader gave him scant encouragement to stay, but grudgingly permitted him to occupy one of the shacks adjoining the native quarters.

So a month had passed. Then, one hot, sun-beaten morning, a long slim graceful schooner had slipped through the passage into the beautiful lagoon, and had dropped her anchor close to the fringing reef, in six fathoms of the best holding ground to be found. Five minutes later, Johnson the trader, received one of the biggest surprises of his life.

While he was still watching the strange schooner manoeuvring for anchorage, the man who had arrived a month before rushed from the shack he had been occupying, and raced across the hot sand, until he reached the spot where the trader stood.

The latter turned slowly and, to his astonishment, found himself gazing into the barrel of a heavy automatic.

"What the —" he began.

"Look here, Johnson," interrupted the other, curtly bending his eyes fiercely upon the trader. "I want you to listen to me and, believe me, you had better hearken well for I am in a hurry. You see that schooner out there?"

"Of course not," answered the trader sarcastically, for he was no coward. "I have been looking through these glasses at the rising moon."

"Don't get funny," snarled the other. "It is just possible that there may be people aboard her who are looking for me."

"I thought you were a fugitive from justice," grunted the trader. "Well, what about it?"

"This about it. I am going into the bush until she leaves. If they ask if a man has arrived here you will say no. If you tell them I am here, I swear to you I will fill you full of lead when I come out of the bush.

"On the other hand, if you stand by me, I will pay you more when I come back than you make here in a year. Don't forget. If you betray me you might as well make your will while you have time."

With that he turned and sped back towards his shack, from which the trader saw him emerge almost at once, and make off into the near by bush.

"The cursed renegade!" he muttered, as he again lifted the glasses. "I thought he was a crook when he landed. So he thinks he can scare me into protecting his dirty hide, does he? And then he wakes up! I'll keep mum just long enough to hear what the people on the schooner have to say. Then I shall use my own discretion."

He calmly continued his contemplation of the ship until he saw a boat lowered and a couple of seamen tumble in, followed by three other figures. As the boat approached the beach, he strolled leisurely to meet it, noticing, as he did so, that the three last figures who had entered were those of two men and a youth. One he sized up with practised eye as being the captain; the other two he could not place.

When the nose of the boat touched the sand, he caught the rope which one of the seamen tossed to him, and held it steady until they had all tumbled out. It was the man he had taken for the captain of the schooner who spoke first.

"Good-morning, Mr. Johnson?"

The trader nodded.

"That is my name."

"And I suppose you are wondering how I know it?" laughed the captain, a breezy old salt, whose skin was almost the colour of coffee. "I got it from Captain Bill Morgan who sails your trading schooner the 'Polly.' I met him in Port Moresby, and when I said I was coming here he told me it was your headquarters."

The trader thawed. Any friend of Bill Morgan's must be all right.

"That is introduction enough," he said extending his hand. "Will you and your friends come up to the house?"

"In a moment, perhaps, Mr. Johnson. Let me first introduce my companions. This" —and he indicated a tall, grave-faced man who stood close to him— "is Mr. John Smith of London. And this" — indicating the youth— "is Master Smith of the same village. Before we accept your hospitality, we think it only fair to tell you why we have come to Rubilinga. We have not come on pleasure."

"Ah!" said the trader non-committally. "Then why have you come?"

"We, or I should say, Mr. Smith, has come after a man whom we have reason to think has come here."

"What makes you think that, skipper?"

The bluff sea-dog turned to the man beside him.

"Here is where you take up the tale, Mr. Smith."

The other smiled slightly, and glanced quizzically at the trader.

"I wonder if I might be perfectly frank with you, Mr. Johnson?"

"I guess there is no danger in it," grunted the trader.

"Very well, I will be. Firstly, let me tell you that I have followed my man from London. He has led me a pretty chase indeed. In South Africa I lost him by one steamer.

"When I reached Melbourne, I found he had gone to Sydney. I wired to the police there, but he slipped through their fingers, and did the same in Brisbane. I followed on, and at Brisbane found the trail led to Thursday Island.

"In Brisbane I chartered the schooner you see in the lagoon here, and followed to Thursday Island. There I lost the trail, but after beating about for some days, decided to try Port Moresby in Papua on a chance.

"Luck was with me, for when I got there, I found that my man was there. I made my arrangements for his arrest, but he must have got wind of them in some way, for he escaped.

"Through a native I discovered he had made for the Solomon Islands in a small boat. Knowing how useless it would be to search aimlessly for him in this archipelago, we waited in Port Moresby. Our patience was rewarded for, finally, through our spies, we discovered that the boat he had taken had returned with the natives who had sailed it.

"Then Captain Weeks here took charge of matters. First he persuaded the natives, by means of his own, to tell him where they had left the white man who had travelled with them. Then he met Captain Morgan, and discovered from him that you were at Rubilinga.

"So, with that information, we set sail, and here we are. Now then, Mr. Johnson, after hearing the story, will you tell us if our information is correct? Has our man landed here, and if so, is he still here?"

The trader turned and let his gaze rove over the lagoon for some minutes; then he looked straight into the eyes of Mr. Smith.

"Before I answer any of your questions I want to know one thing," he said gruffly. "What did this man do?"

"I will tell you that with pleasure. He broke into a bank in London, blew up the safe, shot the watchman dead, and got away with fifty thousand pounds. I want him for that job, and I needn't add, Mr. Johnson, that I am going to stick on his trail until I get home."

"I guess a man who follows his quarry from London to Rubilinga in the South Sea Islands, as you have done, means what he says," grunted the trader. "Now I will answer your question. A man landed here a month ago, and was standing beside me when the schooner entered the lagoon."

"Then he is at the house now?" asked the captain.

The trader shook his head.

"No! The last I saw of him he was disappearing into the bush. He was afraid the schooner held danger for him, and threatened me with a dose of lead if I gave him away. I reckoned he was a crook, but wasn't sure.

"But if he makes friends with the bush natives you will never get him. Not a whole regiment could get him. They can hide him and keep him safe for years, if necessary. The only way to beat him is by strategy, but I have lived here for years, and I can't tell you how."

"Perhaps we can figure out some scheme to beat his game," smiled Mr. Smith.

Then he turned to the captain, and a look passed between them. Immediately the skipper stepped forward a pace.

"I guess, with your help, Mr. Johnson, we can get him. When I tell you the real name of my companion, I think you will agree with me. This gentleman's name is not Smith, but Mr. Sexton Blake of London, and this lad is his assistant, Tinker."

BLACK McCABE,

the missing criminal.

THE SECOND CHAPTER. *Sexton Blake's Magic —Into the Forest.*

IT would be difficult to put into words a description of the consternation which was portrayed on the countenance of the trader, when the skipper revealed the identity of his companions.

It must be remembered that Captain Bill Morgan, of the trader's own schooner, was almost the only white man the latter saw from one year's end to another, Rubilinga was well out of the way of such haphazard traffic as passed amongst the Solomons, and, in fact, not very many people actually knew of its existence.

Bearing this in mind, it can be understood to some extent why Johnson the trader should feel his small universe tumbling about his ears so to speak. In the first place a stranger had burst in upon his quiet life, and now he knew him to be a desperate criminal.

Next had come a slim graceful schooner bearing more strangers, whom he had discovered to be hunting for the first arrival, and one of whom he was now asked to believe was a world-famed London detective.

Had Captain Weeks calmly announced that his companion was the Kaiser Wilhelm or the President of the United States, the trader could not have been more surprised. He gazed at Blake in utter stupefaction for some minutes, then he grinned feebly.

"I guess you are getting at me, captain," he said, looking at the latter for any signs that he was being made the victim of a joke.

"I tell you it is on the level, Johnson. He is the man I say he is."

"Scott! The man you are after must be big meat for you to hang on to his trail so hard, Mr. Blake," grunted the trader.

Blake, for it was really he, smiled.

"He is, Mr. Johnson; but even if he were much smaller meat I should still stick. It is a matter of professional pride with me to land him."

"Well, I am quite willing to believe that he is the man you are after," rejoined Johnson. "He looks equal to most anything; but let me tell you it is going to be no cinch to catch him on this island.

"You have no idea what it means to cut your way through the undergrowth, and, as I said before, if he makes it up with the hill tribes, and they choose to protect him, you might as well give up at once.

"I am quite willing to do all I can to help you, but I doubt if I can persuade any niggers to go into the bush with you. These coast boys have a perpetual feud with the mountain tribes, and a meeting between them is a signal for a fight, and a fight means a general slaughter."

"I am quite sure you will do all you can to help us," answered Blake. "If we can get some of your boys together, so much the better; but if not, we must do without. In that case, I shall have to go in alone, for if my man has taken to the bush, there I go, too."

"And into certain death," said the trader curtly. "You don't understand what it means, Mr. Blake. Why, that jungle back there is swarming with death in a hundred different forms, from the natives, who can pick you off from ambush, down to the black snakes which abound, and which mean certain death in fifteen seconds if they bite you."

"I realise to the full just what the dangers are," replied Blake quietly; "but if you are prepared to lend us your advice, Mr. Johnson, suppose we move on to your house? Then you can ask your boys if any of them will accompany us."

They all turned and moved along the beach passing beneath the coconut-trees which fringed it, and keeping on until they reached the stockade.

On arriving at the shack which the trader called his house, the new arrivals sat down in the shade of the rough verandah, and sipped appreciatively at the cooling homemade brew which the trader served them. Then they sat and waited until a boy went to fetch the foreman of Johnson's negroes.

When he arrived he proved to be a big, sinister-looking Rubilingan, whom one could well believe capable of all the deeds attributed to the tribe of which he was a member.

He stood before them while the trader addressed him in pidgin English for some moments.

When Johnson had finished speaking the native turned his eyes on Blake, then spoke rapidly in reply.

As his voice died away the trader turned to Blake.

"He says it will be impossible to get together a party of men to accompany you. He says that he himself would be willing to go, but that none would accompany him.

"He says further, that two of the hill tribes have joined forces, and that should a party venture in from here they would be annihilated."

"What does he think of the man who has taken refuge there?" asked Blake.

The trader turned, and again spoke to the Rubilingan; then he answered:

"He says the white man who sought the bush may go unharmed because he has the evil eye and knows much magic."

Then his voice dropped.

"And that tells me something I didn't know before," he added quickly. "It means he has been meddling with my niggers. If I had dreamed that anything like that was going on I would have shot him. He has evidently impressed them in some way."

"Very easy for him," said Blake. "He is an accomplished hypnotist, I believe. In his hands your boys would be as putty."

"For two pins I would drive them into the bush at the point of a gun and make them go on!" snapped the trader. "Only they would run away at the first chance. Anyway, until my schooner comes back I don't dare leave. They would loot the place and burn it down. By the way, Captain Weeks, what have you in the shape of a crew?"

"Two white men. Been with me for years. They work on shares, and will have to remain in charge of the schooner. The rest of the crew are all Kanakas, and no good for this proposition."

The trader wrinkled his brows in deep thought, then turned to Blake.

"Believe me, Mr. Blake, I'd like very much to help you, but I don't see what I can do."

"I quite understand your position, Mr. Johnson," answered Blake; "but don't worry. A plan has occurred to me, and if we move quickly we may overtake our man before he has had time to seek sanctuary with any of the bush tribes. Tinker, step back to the boat at once. Go on board the schooner, get Pedro, and return at once."

With an understanding look in his eyes Tinker shot away in the direction of the beach. While he was gone Blake explained his plan, and as he unfolded it a look of deep admiration came into the eyes of the trader.

"By thunder! Mr. Blake, you have hit on the only solution of it. The danger is in no way lessened, but your chances of success are increased. Your man can't be very far away, and, unless he strikes natives before night, he will have to pull up.

"Besides, I don't think he will anticipate being followed, and certainly not in the way you suggest. Scott! Who would believe it? A man hunt in the jungle of Rubilinga, with a London bloodhound on the trail. I am beginning to think my solitude has been killed for ever."

"I can tell you one thing," put in the skipper at this juncture. "I am about as much at home in the bush as a dolphin would be in Piccadilly, but you can count me in on this thing."

"This will be first rate," said Blake. "That will make two of us without the lad and the dog. Tinker is worth any three niggers who may be pitted against us, and Pedro is as good as any white man. We will hope, however, that we can overtake our man before he reaches any tribal village."

"I suppose you will wait until to-morrow morning, and get an early start?" asked the trader.

Blake smiled.

"I know it seems foolhardy to start off into the jungle so precipitately, but, in my opinion, a speedy start means a quicker success. If our quarry could risk it, then we can."

"And when the Government agent goes through the bush, he does so with half a hundred carriers and as many fighting men," breathed the trader.

"Which is exactly why a lone man of commonsense can risk it without a big party," rejoined Blake. "The impression caused by the passage of the Government agent with his train of carriers is remembered, and the white man's colour makes him important in their eyes."

"Not always, when they have as short a memory as have most of the Rubilinga head hunters," grunted the trader. "However, if you are determined to start at once, I will do all I can to help you. You have your own arms and ammunition, I suppose?"

"Yes. If you will get together some tinned meat and biscuits, some rice, tea, sugar, and trade goods, I think that will be all. I should suggest that you arrange loads for about six carriers."

"But where will you get the carriers?" asked Johnson.

Blake did not answer at once; but, reaching into his pocket, drew out one of the powerful pocket lenses without which he never travelled.

"I remember once in South America I got stuck for carriers," he drawled. "I offered the Indians what to them represented a fortune; but something had driven fear into them, and not all the beads or cheap hardware in the world would move them.

"I drew out a pocket-glass, and by accident discovered that I had struck something which awed them as nothing else did. Twenty cheap pocket magnifying-glasses made them my slaves for life. Now, with your permission, Mr. Johnson, I am going to see if the same trick will overcome the fear which seems to have been instilled in your 'boys.'"

The trader looked on with interest, while the captain chuckled in the depths of his salty beard.

Gravely Blake stepped forward, holding the glass in his hand. He paused for a moment before the black foreman, who was regarding him with a puzzled look. Then, so gently that the black was hardly aware of what he was doing, Blake took the knotted hand, and raised it as high as the waist. With his right hand he brought the pocket-glass into position until the lens was in a direct line with the blazing sun.

The Rubilingan bent in silent obedience to the command of Blake's eyes, and his own dusky orbs widened a trifle as he saw the strange forest which appeared through the glass.

He had not intelligence enough to realise that the giant stems at which he was looking were the hairs on the back of his own hand, for a brain which is only capable of counting up to twenty, and that by using the fingers and toes as counters, is not advanced enough to grasp the intricacies of the concave or convex lens.

He was still regarding the strange phenomena with wondering gaze when suddenly he jerked his hand from Blake's grasp, and shot up into the air with a startled yell.

When he came back to earth he was nursing his hand and glaring at the glass with angry fright. It was his first experience with the burning power of a magnifying-glass.

Blake never relaxed his grave expression as he beckoned to the native, and walked a few steps to where grew a few spears of withered grass. Bending, he pulled them up by the roots, and made a small pile of them. Then, once more adjusting the glass so the lens caught the sun; he made an imperative gesture for the native to draw closer.

Thoroughly imbued with the mystery of the thing, the black did so. For a few minutes nothing happened; but, when a little later, the dry grass began to smoke, and finally broke into a blaze, he dropped to the ground with a whimper and touched his forehead to Blake's feet.

His conquest was complete, and it was evident that in the man before him he recognised a greater magician than the man who had gone into the bush. That being so, he had no more to fear from the latter, for who could prevail against a man who could produce a forest before one's eyes, who could sear the flesh on one's hand, and who could wave a small object about and cause fire where no fire had been?

Truly he must be a far greater sorcerer than any the Rubilinga tribes possessed. So reasoned the primitive mind of the native, and such reasoning had Blake anticipated.

Raising the black to his feet, Blake turned to the trader.

"Now, Mr. Johnson," he said, "will you tell him I desire that he shall secure five of his fellows and accompany me into the bush? You might say that if he refuses I shall be very angry, and will let him feel my anger, which will be quite true, for if he refuses I shall be tempted to pull his sooty nose for him."

The trader could scarcely repress his amusement as he turned to the black, and said sternly:

"The great white sorcerer commands you to procure five of your fellows and accompany him into the bush. You have nothing to fear from the one who has gone. This magician is much more powerful, and will protect you; but if you refuse he will be very angry."

The black gave one fearful look at Blake, then stuttered in his pidgin English:

"Me get felloh quick now, boss. All ready, yes."

With that he sped away, and the trio of white men laughed heartily.

"Scott!" exclaimed the trader. "I have been living amongst these people for sixteen years, and that trick never occurred to me."

"A burning glass is one of the most puzzling things to the primitive mind," rejoined Blake as he drew a cigarette. "I imagine we shall have no difficulty about carriers, and unless I am greatly mistaken here comes Tinker and Pedro and, I think, yes, I am sure, he is bringing the arms with him."

An hour later when the six carriers had been loaded and headed for the jungle, Blake took Pedro's leash and led him to the shack so recently occupied by the man he was hunting.

Then, with Pedro on the trail, the dog's leash in one hand and his automatic in the other, he broke into the jungle on what he hoped would be the last lap of his long man hunt. Tinker swung in behind him, the carriers followed, and Captain Weeks with drawn revolver brought up the rear.

And, prepared though they were for almost anything, not one of them dreamed in the slightest degree what surprises Fate had in store for them when next they saw the trading station on the edge of the Rubilinga lagoon.

On arriving at the hut Blake lit his pipe, and, after
seating himself, motioned to Abonga to stand
before him.

WHEN Henry Johnson, the Rubilingan trader, waved his hand to the little expedition which had set off into the jungle and turned back to his shack he felt, that for a time at least, he could go about his business undisturbed.

It was just on two in the afternoon when the dense undergrowth had swallowed up the party, and in the ordinary course of events the trader ought now to be sunk in slumber. A midday siesta is a necessity in Rubilinga.

The fitting out of the expedition, however, had upset his usual routine, and a small batch of natives who should have been attended to during the morning were still lying about in the shadow cast by the store, chewing betel nut and waiting to be served. Consequently the trader was compelled to give up all idea of a nap and attend to them.

They bore the usual burdens of shell, copra and cinchona bark, and, to the tired trader, seemed even more leisurely than usual in their choice of trade goods.

Perfectly good axes, which were invariably seized upon with avidity, they passed by with a glance and worried about amongst the cheap knives and other smaller hardware.

Brilliantly tinted cloth, which they usually sought eagerly for making perineal bands and skirts, held no attractions for them; but a cheap line of nickel watches which the trader had received held them spellbound. So the weary hours passed, and to the trader it seemed as if their choice would never be made.

Now the Solomon Island savage is a being identified with Nature almost as closely as the birds and beasts of his native haunts. He is very, very far indeed below the white man in the scales of civilisation.

He has never known anything different from his present home. His ideas are as primitive as they were before the white man ever invaded his retreat, and only in the immediate vicinity of the white man's buildings does the latter's influence show.

Even on the other side of the Rubilinga lagoon the natives are quite as primitive as ever, and, though the dread of the white man has caused them to give up open cannibalism, it is still carried on secretly.

Their habits and customs are still the same. The perineal band, formerly of beaten bark cloth, but now, at least in the vicinity of the trading stations of trade cloth, still forms the only article of clothing.

The tribal sorcerer still rules supreme, keeping at bay the myriad of ghosts, which, to the Rubilingan mind, are the cause of all bad fortune, They still tip their spears with stone and pierce their ears. The custom of nose boring is general, and even the snake ceremony in connection with that performance still holds sway.

Their houses are mere sapling shacks built in temporary clearings in the forest. Nomadic by nature, they move on frequently, and it is not long before the spreading jungle has almost obliterated the sight of the previous village.

The single men and boys still live in "club-houses," and the tribal wars still continue. So do they exist as they have always existed, and if the passing white man sees little of their true life it is not because these things do not exist, but because they regard all intruders as hostile.

Consequently, it can be readily seen how such utter children of nature must be most sensitive to all her moods. And Henry Johnson, the Australian trader, had not spent sixteen years amongst the Solomon Islands without knowing this.

He knew something was causing their listless attitude towards the regular trade goods and making them irritatingly changeable in their desires. All the while he was guiding their childish minds towards the goods he wished to dispose of he was studying them surreptitiously.

At first he thought some tribal feud must have broken out and that their minds were elsewhere. But the undoubted friendliness of the rival clans who were there precluded this idea and made him seek further for an answer.

It was only when an errand took him outside the gloomy store into the glare of the afternoon sun that he had his answer. On coming into the open air he was at once struck by the oppressiveness of the atmosphere.

Glancing up sharply he saw that a sickly yellow haze was slowly-creeping over the blue dome, and, on casting an anxious eye out to sea, he saw that the blue water was more like grey, sleeky oil. The sun glared balefully through its yellow veil, and behind him the jungle seemed full of brooding menace.

Even as he gazed about him birds broke cover and wheeled shrieking overhead. The tame pigs about the village rooted listlessly, yet kept near their retreats. The stiff leaves of the coconut palms rustled uncannily in the heavy air; the schooner in the lagoon seemed anchored in oil.

All nature was weighed down with heavy foreboding. And only too readily did the trader read the reason. The monsoon was about to break, a deluge was promised, and from the absolute veracity of Nature's barometer he knew it was to be of the sternest description.

So much he read outside, and now he knew the reason for the attitude of the natives. Even, though they had been in the shop for hours, they too, felt the oppression, and like the birds and beasts and trees, reflected it in their actions.

He abandoned whatever errand had brought him outside, and, hurrying back into the store, turned out the natives. Then he called his black assistants together and sent them scurrying to bring in everything which was movable.

That done he despatched two men to the schooner to warn the sailors in charge that a hurricane was imminent, and when they had gone he went to his shack and completed his preparations there. The natives had dispersed long since, and, those in his employ had sought their huts.

Just before sundown the trader stood on his low verandah and cast a careful eye about him. As far as he could see everything had been done that could be done to meet the deluge which promised.

The schooner had been pulled round under the lee of the shore and her poles had been stripped. With hatches battened down and an additional anchor out astern she looked fairly well prepared to ride out the storm.

With a last anxious look in the direction of his coconut palms the trader turned back into his shack. And that night the same storm which had struck the steamship Kara Maru farther to the west swept down upon the Solomons in all its fury.

Thanks to the trader's preparations the little trading station on Rubilinga withstood the blast bravely, and though Johnson kept a careful eye out all the next day he could see no damage of any great amount.

True, some of his coconut palms had been levelled as though a giant scythe had swept through them, and the broad leaves of the banana trees had been cut to ribbons before the trees themselves went down. But, so far, the shacks had stood up under it, and if they could weather the worst of the blast they were safe.

One could hardly imagine that the boiling cauldron in front of the station had only a few hours before been a lagoon of soft azure. Even though protected by the barrier reef of the atoll it had been whipped into a lake of yellow foam by the hurricane, and, looking at it with the land circling it, one could imagine what the sea beyond must be like.

Torrents of rain were hurtling down, and as yet the heavens showed no signs of breaking. Johnson thought anxiously of the little expedition which had set off into the bush and wondered how they were faring.

Thanks to his warning, the schooner's preparations had been sufficient, and, though she was tossing about like a cork in the lagoon, her holding anchors still held fast. Several times throughout the day the two sailors on board had signalled all well, and that night the trader retired with an easier mind.

Dawn was just breaking when he arose and again went outside to see what the damage had been during the night. Though to the casual observer the storm appeared worse, the trader's practised eye knew it for the last defiant blast before the change.

He noticed with satisfaction that all the huts still stood and that the schooner had ridden out the night safely. It was while he was looking at her that he saw something which caused him to knit his brows in puzzlement.

He could see the figures of the two seamen on deck. They appeared to be preparing to hoist something to the mast-head and must have seen him too, for one of them waved his arm wildly.

Calling through the door the trader told a native boy to bring him his glasses. He trained them on the schooner and watched while the sailors shook out a string of flags and began pulling on the rope.

As they went upwards and stiffened out in the wind the trader read the signal and whistled in surprise. It ran:

"Wreck outside, one survivor, will try get boat ashore, be ready to help."

Hardly able to believe his senses, Johnson read the message a second time, then calling a boy, sent him scurrying towards the huts. A few minutes later half a dozen natives came out on the run, and obeying the trader's command, followed him to the beach. Even as they reached the strip of sand they saw that a boat was being lowered on the lee side of the schooner.

The first attempt at launching was doomed to failure, for the boat was lifted up by a wave and tossed inwards with a sweep which threatened to crush it like an eggshell. Only the frantic efforts of the Kanakas on board saved it.

At the second attempt however, they met with success, and the little party on the beach watched closely while the two white sailors lowered another man into the boat and followed after. Then they pushed off and laid to the oars with a will.

Only when they topped the crest of a wave would the trader see them, but as they drew nearer and nearer to the shore he saw they had a good chance of making it safely. When they were still some twenty yards away he issued a curt command to the natives.

They dashed into the water as he spoke and parted, forming a lane through which the boat could come. And a moment later she came like an arrow. Caught up by a huge wave she poised for a second on its crest, then straight for the beach she shot.

Between the two lines of natives she came and sent her nose into the sand. Before the hungry wave could snatch her back the natives had her by the gunwale and had run her up on the beach.

The trader hurried forward now and met the seamen as they hopped out.

"I read your message all right," he said. "I could hardly believe it. Do you mean to tell me there has been a wreck outside the reef?"

The elder of the two sailors nodded.

"Yes, sir, and from what I can make out from the single survivor it has been a bad one. I'll tell you what I know, then you can talk to him. He is pretty weak yet.

"It was about two hours ago that one of the Kanakas who was on watch woke us and told us he had seen the port light of a steamer out at sea, and that she appeared to be driving towards the island.

"My mate and I went on deck at once, but could see nothing. We thought the Kanaka had been dreaming. However we kept a sharp look-out, and half an hour later saw the light he had spoken of. It was close to the reef then, and things looked bad for the ship to which it belonged.

"I at once sent up a couple of rockets, but saw none in reply. I also fired off a gun several times to try to attract your attention, but I guess the noise was lost in the wind.

"For us to launch a boat was out of the question; all we could do was to keep a look-out and wait for dawn. Another half an hour passed, and we saw nothing further of the light.

"We were just reckoning the ship had passed the island safely when we heard a cry which seemed to come from the lagoon. I sent one of the Kanakas for lantern and held it over the side, shouting as I did so.

"I was sure the cry I had heard was a trick of the storm, so you can imagine how I felt when my shout was answered. This time the cry was close to the schooner, and a few seconds later I saw a man straggling in the water.

"We heaved over a rope, which he caught, and pulled him aboard. He was about all in, but I guess he will be all right soon. We didn't bother him much with questions, but he told us a little of his own accord.

"Says he is the only survivor of the steamship Kara Maru, bound from Brisbane to Hong Kong. He was a seaman aboard her. He says the hurricane struck them about two days ago near the Great Barrier, and that they lost their propeller.

"They were swept along before it, and went on the reef in the night. He put a lifebelt round him, and jumped just as she went down. I don't know how he ever found the passage into the lagoon and made it, but he did, and kept up until we heard him.

"That is all I know, sir; but if his story is true, the loss of life must have been heavy. I know the Kara Mara, and she would have a full list."

The astounded trader nodded.

"Yes, I know her, too. It seems incredible; but I will talk with the survivor. He seems pretty weak, but I shall soon pull him round."

He stepped close to the boat as he spoke, and looked down at the big, bearded man who lay in the bottom leaning weakly against a seat.

"Pretty well knocked up, are you?" he asked cheerily.

The man in the boat nodded and answered huskily.

"You say the Kara Mara drove on the reefs here last night?"

"Yes; I think I am the only survivor. She went ashore to the west of the lagoon passage."

"How on earth did you ever get through there in that hurricane?"

"I don't know. I jumped over just before she went under. The passengers and crew were fighting at the boats. I saw a break in the line of foam and swam for it. I got into the lagoon somehow, and held up until they threw me a rope from the schooner."

"Were there many passengers on board?"

"A full list."

"Were you a seaman?"

"Yes; I joined her at Sydney."

"Your name?"

"William Carr."

"All right. If you feel well enough to walk, come with me, I will give you some warm clothes, and fix you up as well as possible, here, you!" He called to a couple of natives. "Take this man up to the shack which was occupied by the other white man. Hurry up. I will be right along!"

When the two natives had helped the bearded man from the boat, and had assisted him along the beach, the trader turned to the remaining natives and gave them some rapid orders. Then he turned and accompanied by the seamen, followed the survivor to the huts.

Almost at the same instant that they entered the stockade the rain stopped, and with that incredible swiftness peculiar to the tropics, the sky began to clear. Already the lagoon was growing less violent, and the trader realised with satisfaction that in a few more hours the sea itself would become normal.

They entered the shack where the natives had taken the survivor, and saw that he had dropped down upon the rough couch which stood against the wall.

The trader sent one of the boys to his own shack for warm clothing, food, and spirits, and half an hour later the worn-out man, who had come to Rubilinga in such a strange manner, was sleeping quietly.

Johnson and the two sailors then returned to the beach and stood by the boat until they saw the four natives who had gone on at the trader's bidding, break through the coconut palms on the far side of the lagoon and hurry around the circular beach towards them.

Each of them bore burdens of some kind, and as they got closer, the white man could see that they were composed of numerous small articles. They came in at a rapid pace, and held out their burdens for the trader's inspection.

He glanced them over with a practised eye, then his hand shot out and grasped one of the objects.

"By thunder, the man's tale seems true enough!" he said, turning to the sailors and holding up the object he held.

"This is the back of a deck-chair, and you can see here the name Kara Mara. And look here. This lifebuoy also bears her name. Heavens, what a loss!"

Quickly he turned to the natives and talked rapidly with them for some time; then he swung back towards the seamen.

"They say the beach is strewn with wreckage, and that they brought it here as I directed. They say there is no sign of the steamer, but that they can see where she struck. She has probably slipped off into deep water."

"Did they find any bodies, sir?"

Johnson shook his head.

"No. And I hardly expected that, either. They say the place is now alive with sharks."

"That explains it then," granted the sailor. "What will you do about it, sir?"

"Well, we must get the news out somehow. My own schooner is away just now, and it will be impossible for you to go without a captain. The nearest island of any size is sixty miles away, but if we can get word to them they can soon send it on, for there is a wireless there.

"I have a heavy whaling-boat, and if one of you will volunteer to take charge of it, I will give you these four natives to work it. I can set you on your way, and you can reach it easily. Besides, two of these fellows have made the trip and know the course. What do you say?"

Both sailors spoke at once.

"Sure, Mr. Johnson, I'm game."

"Well, then, supposing you toss up for it. One of you will have to remain in charge of the schooner, and any extra help he needs I can supply it. The sea will be calm enough to leave by noon, and with the wind in its present quarter, you should reach your destination by nightfall."

The two sailors acquiesced in the trader's plan, and when the coin was tossed it fell to the lot of the younger to make the trip. No time was lost in completing their preparations.

First, the boat was rowed back to the schooner where the one who was to remain was left, and the other collected a few things. Then it returned, and under the direction of the trader the natives launched the big whaleboat.

Slowly and carefully he gave them their instructions, then just as the last stormcloud fled and the sun blazed down with bright promise from the zenith, the boat was pushed off and, under the powerful strokes of the four Rubilingans, shot across the lagoon towards the passage, bound on her mission —a mission which would startle the shipping world of the East.

In the centre of the open space was a large blazing fire, and around this were dancing the women of the tribe in a wild orgy of frenzied shrieking.

The light which Blake flashed on the twisting mass before him
lit up a vicious scene.

THE FOURTH CHAPTER. *A Great Fight.*

OWING to the short start his quarry had, Sexton Blake had hoped, by the assistance of Pedro, to overtake him before he succeeded in getting very far into the bush. Had the weather held, there is no doubt but he would have succeeded in doing so within a day or two; but the hurricane which brought so much damage at sea was also the cause of wrecking his plans.

At first the trail had been easy to follow. Pedro held the scent confidently, and they had not proceeded far before they saw that the fugitive was following a faintly defined path which led directly inland.

More than once during the day they saw signs of his passage in the freshly-cut underbrush, and though they did not succeed in coming up with him, they knew they were on the right trail.

It was absolutely essential to camp that night, for their hunger had to be appeased, and the six carriers must rest. Blake had the camp pitched close to a small stream, and it was a very tired party which threw themselves down immediately after the evening meal of tinned meat and biscuits, washed down with water.

Blake set two-hour watches for himself, Tinker, and the captain, and he it was who took the first one. The hurricane had already struck the island, but, situated as they were in the midst of the dense forest, they did not at first feel the effects of the blast which was even then whipping the lagoon into a boiling, yellow froth.

It was just towards the end of his watch that the rapidly increasing noise of the stream beside which they were camped told Blake that a terrific storm must be raging overhead. Without waking the others, he bent over the bank to examine the stream, and was startled to discover that what had been but a tiny silver ribbon when they pitched camp was already a swollen torrent, rising every second.

Hastily he woke the others, and without delay they shifted the camp farther back. To the superstitious natives this was a bad omen, and was immediately attributed to the evil ghosts controlled by the man they were following.

Only the leader's fear of Blake and the latter's revolver prevented them from bolting off into the night and leaving the whites alone. All hands welcomed the coming of dawn for, during the night a series of terrific crashes, many uncomfortably close to them, told of some forest giant going down under the blast.

Realising that the best way to keep the carriers under control was to load them up and get started, Blake lost no time in breaking camp. They started off again, with Pedro once more in the lead, and Tinker and the captain both bringing up the rear with drawn revolvers.

As they progressed, Blake saw that they were steadily climbing, though slowly. To his surprise, it had hardly been necessary to do any cutting as yet. What hasty strokes had been made by the fugitive permitted them to pass, and Blake was strongly hopeful of overtaking him that day.

Though the quarry would be delayed by the necessity for cutting his way from time to time, that gain to the pursuers was more than offset by the necessary slowness of their progress, for the carriers could not travel with the same speed as an unburdened and fear-driven man.

How the fugitive was procuring his food Blake had only a vague idea. He strongly suspected that a native was guiding the white man, and that the former was securing the necessary food. This was only guesswork on Blake's part, but in the absence of any other suggestion he accepted it.

He was disappointed when the second night overtook them, and still they had seen no signs of their quarry. From the leader of the natives Blake discovered that they were now upon the fringe of the country of the nearest hill tribes, and that already the news of their coming would have been flashed from village to village.

According to the black, they should make the first village the next day. Consequently, Blake chose the situation of his camp that night with care, and impressed upon the others the necessity for a rigid look-out.

His experiences in the South American jungle had taught him much about the savage nature, and when during his own watch that night he heard several faint cries at a great distance, he knew as well as the natives themselves what it meant.

Those who have travelled amongst the savage peoples of the world have one and all been mystified how, through what seems almost impenetrable jungle, news is flashed from one tribe to another.

In some districts this is done by the beating of a drum, the sound travelling a long distance and, in a telegraphic way, telling the one who hears it what it is desired to impart. This one then takes it up and beats out the message to another, still more distant; and so, on it goes over miles of country in a remarkably short time.

In the Solomons the savage tribes have their own special method of sending messages. Amongst the hill tribes it is not the drum which is used, but the human voice.

Standing upon a hill, a native shouts his message across the great valley far to the other hill, where another native is stationed. He in turn takes it up and shouts it to another, and so the message flies from village to village, from tribe to tribe.

And this shouting it was which Blake heard during the night. Well he knew what it meant, and well he realised that, though they had seen no one on their journey, invisible eyes had watched them from the depths of the forest, and had sent the news of their coming far over the hills.

That meant they had also watched the coming of the fugitive, and were he successful in his advances he might even now be resting secure in one of their villages.

If that were so, Blake realised he would indeed have his work cut out for him, and that, before they again emerged from the forest, they might see more than one strenuous hour. And such anticipation was to be fulfilled far more than he reckoned on.

Tinker relieved him at midnight, and the lad in his turn was relieved by the captain at two. When the latter woke Blake again at four, he had nothing to report so, again taking the watch, Blake watched anxiously for the dawn.

It came, and with it a lull in the storm. After a meagre breakfast Blake drove the carriers to their loads, and again started on. All morning they laboured through the dense undergrowth, finding it far more tangled than they had at any time since starting.

It was hard on midday when suddenly they burst forth into a clearing, and saw before them half a dozen native huts. It was the village of which the leader of Blake's carriers had spoken.

Pedro's training was proof enough that Black McCabe, the man Blake was after, had come that way, and, knowing the criminal as he did know him, Blake was prepared for any hostile move.

Black McCabe, be it known, was a new, but none the less desperate, planet which had swum into the criminal firmament of

London, and for some months had been carrying on his operations unchecked.

His boast that neither Scotland Yard nor Sexton Blake could catch him had reached Blake's ears, and therein lay the reason of Blake's taking up of the challenge. His long chase after Blake McCabe is no part of this story.

Sufficient is it to say that Blake had stuck to the trail from London to South Africa, from South Africa to Australia, from Australia to Thursday Island, from Thursday Island to Port Moresby in New Guinea, and from there to Rubilinga. And having started out to get his man, he was determined not to go back without him.

It was quite probable that Black McCabe's hypnotic ability had overcome the hostility of the mountain clan which resided in the village they had reached, and knowing McCabe would not stop at a general slaughter of his pursuers if it would serve his purpose, Blake decided to move cautiously.

At first glance one might have thought the village uninhabited. Not a native was to be seen, and only the village pig, which rooted about told of human occupation.

The half-dozen huts were scattered about in a disordered fashion. A large one in the centre Blake took to be that of the chief, and, at one side he could see the open end of the village club-house, the open-ended shack existing in all Solomon Island villages, where the boys and men of the tribe are wont to sleep.

Blake knew enough of the etiquette of the savages to know that the club-house must be first approached, so, after a consultation with the others, he broke cover and started across the open towards it.

As he strode forward, Blake knew perfectly well that dozens of eyes were probably watching him, and that a dozen spears might come hurtling forth at any moment. But if he felt nervous he gave no sign, and on arriving at the club, saw his suspicions were correct.

In the gloom he could see row after row of men and boys, their eyes peering forth at him with silent menace. Curtly Blake made a gesture for the foreman of his own natives to step forward, and with him as interpreter, opened the interview.

"Where is the chief?" he asked.

The leader of the carriers put the question, and when a guttural voice had answered him, he turned back to Blake. He spoke in pidgin

English, but so crude and complicated were his phrases that for the purpose of clarity, his replies are given in ordinary English.

"He says he is the chief, and asks what you want," he said to Blake.

"Tell him we desire food and a place to sleep," answered Blake. "Say that we come as friends, and that we bring presents and goods to pay for what we receive."

The native did as he was bid, but when he interpreted the chief's reply, he did so haltingly.

"He says he has no need of presents, and that he does not wish strangers in the village."

"You tell him that I have come here as a friend, and that he will be punished if he refuses his hospitality," snapped Blake.

Perhaps the chief realised the meaning of Blake's tones, for without waiting for the interpretation he spoke again.

"He says he will give you a vacant hut," translated the carrier; "but that he hopes you will move on soon. He asks again why you have come."

"Ask him if another man has passed this way," said Blake curtly.

"He says he has not seen any white man for many months, and that none has passed this way."

Blake turned to Tinker and Captain Weeks.

"Look here!" he said quietly. "McCabe has come here, we know. Pedro could not make a mistake. In some way he has managed to swing these people to his side, and the old chief is lying.

"McCabe may even now be skulking at the back of them, or in one of the huts. I am determined to stick to him until I land him, so my suggestion is, that we accept the offer of the hut and talk things over. What do you say?"

"Whatever you suggest goes to me," said the captain quickly. "I am here to obey orders."

"Me, too," chimed in Tinker, with a cheerful disregard for grammar.

Blake turned to the black.

"Tell him we accept his offer of a hut, and that we desire to go to it at once. This evening we will open our packs and send him our presents."

The carrier talked with the chief for a few moments, then, turning back to Blake, he pointed to a hut near the edge of the village.

"That is the hut," he said.

"Very well. Take the bundles over there. We follow."

They made their way to the hut which had been indicated, and for half an hour were busy disposing of their belongings.

Then, while the blacks curled up and went to sleep, Blake held a council of war.

To say the least, the little party of whites were in a far from desirable situation.

Over thirty miles of dense jungle separated them from the nearest white man, and he had his hands full where he was. Then came sixty miles of blue ocean before another white settlement, and they, like Johnson the trader, had their own troubles.

Government troops or assistance were not to be had, and, even were they near, they would have been refused, for the powers that be have a habit of frowning upon independent expeditions in the Solomons. So they had none but themselves and their own ingenuity to depend upon.

Get the position. There they were, isolated in a village of savage and cannibalistic Rubilingans. Behind them lay the jungle, with no assistance to lessen its terrors. Before them lay more jungle and other villages, more savage even than the one they were in —savage because further removed from the shadow of the white man.

To make matters worse, the renegade white man whom they were chasing had reached the village before them, and in some way had influenced the savages in his favour. Had a black been the quarry, such a thing would not have mattered so much, but no one realised better than Blake what a dangerous example it was for the savages to see white men at loggerheads.

And be sure Black McCabe, the criminal, would not consider the higher ethics in his efforts to outwit his pursuers. Whether it was the hypnotic eye he was credited with having, or by some other means Blake did not know, but if Pedro's guidance was to be trusted, then it seemed a foregone conclusion that Black McCabe was not only in the same village but within a stone's throw of them.

The psychology of relations between black man and white man is not easy to treat, but it is a fact that the inherently evil white man is more freely accepted by the savage than is the more honourable white man.

The savageness of nature which prompts the criminal to perform his deeds of darkness may find a bond of sympathy in the primitive nature of the savage. That one cannot tell.

Whatever the cause, this much was certain. Black McCabe was in the village, and, to all intents and purposes, in command of the situation. Therefore Blake saw that he should need all his own cunning to undermine McCabe's influence and turn the tables on the renegade.

On the other hand, if McCabe should become inflamed, then he might strike first, and, should he do so, Blake realised that the apparently peaceful village might run with blood before the thing was over.

To avoid such an occurrence he concentrated all his mind and brought to bear all the experience he had ever had with savage peoples. It took some time for him to outline all his plans to Tinker and Captain Weeks, and when the three finally rose from the council, the sun had already set behind the trees to the west.

Roughly stated, Blake's plan was this.

First, the bundles would be unpacked, and a distribution of gifts made to the tribe. After that, Blake would himself present a special assortment of articles to the chief, and when the grand pow-wow was over, endeavour to find out how the land lay.

If his attempts failed, they would then wait for morning, and if by then the chief had given them no satisfaction, Blake would boldly demand that the white man be handed over to him. If this also failed, then another line of argument must be used.

All hands turned to and unpacked the bundles of trade goods, and when they had all been arranged, Blake sent the leader of his own blacks to summon the villagers. They came en masse, and, once within the hut where the trade goods were displayed, seemed to lose all the surly restraint they had exhibited when the party arrived and became the children they really were.

One by one Blake had them led past him, and as each went by handed him a knife or axe, piece of cloth, and some trade tobacco. For the chief he had reserved a particularly fine axe, a large roll of red cotton, five pounds of trade tobacco, a collection of beads, and a large, loud-ticking American alarm clock.

These he laid to one side, and when the last of the tribe had departed with his gifts, Blake called one of his blacks and loaded him up with the chief's gifts. Then, with the captain and Tinker acting as bodyguard, he made his way across the open space in the middle of the village towards the chief's house.

On his return to his own hut Blake had to confess himself disappointed with the result of the pow-wow. The chief had apparently been perfectly friendly, and had accepted the gifts with many protestations of life-long friendship.

But to all Blake's questions he had returned evasive answers, and, through it all, Blake felt the chief was playing a part. He was irritated that Black McCabe should wield so much silent power, for not a sign had he seen of that individual.

Yet the unvoiced opposition with which he met only made him more determined than ever to beat the renegade, and when he gave it up for that night, it was with the stern resolve that he should gain a trick on the morrow.

Though his ears were still ringing with the friendly utterances of the chief, Blake was not taken in to the extent of abolishing his nightly system of watches.

So when the little hut on the outskirts of the village finally gave itself up to slumber, Blake himself was squatting by the smouldering embers near the doorway, listening to the night cries of the surrounding jungle, and wondering if Black McCabe would follow up his victory of the day by making some move during the night.

It was getting towards the end of his watch, when Blake heard a faint noise which he knew instinctively was not of the jungle. It seemed to be just outside the hut, and at first he took it for one of the village pigs.

He leant forward, and strained his ears, listening. After a few moments it stopped, and while he might have counted a hundred silence reigned. Then it came again, and this time Blake's keen hearing detected it even closer than before.

Without a sound on his own part he rose and stole softly across the hut to where Tinker and the captain lay sleeping. As he bent to shake them, he felt a cold muzzle pressed against his hand, and knew Pedro had heard the noise, too.

He breathed a guarded warning in his companions' ears as he woke them, and in a few whispered words told them why he had roused them. They rose at once, and all three crept back towards the entrance.

Barely had they reached it, and ensconced themselves on either side of the opening when a faint whistling noise came through the night. A second later there was a sharp swish close to them, and a long slim spear flew through the opening to land with a soft punk in the mud floor.

As though that were a signal of some sort half a dozen more came hurtling through the darkness, some burying themselves in the plaited grass walls of the hut, and others following the first.

One reached the corner where the carriers lay sleeping, bringing them to their feet with startled exclamations. At the same instant the dark and apparently sleeping village leaped into a blazing, shrieking, dancing pandemonium of bloodthirsty savages.

Six black shadows flashed past the men at the door as the carriers, in a panic, deserted en masse, and tore off into the bush, leaving the little band of whites to face the crisis alone. And as they stared out grimly at the scene, even Blake's heart fell.

The whole village was lit up by the fires, which had been lighted simultaneously. In the centre of the open space was one larger than the rest, and around this were dancing the women of the tribe in a wild orgy of frenzied shrieking.

Their bodies had been oiled until they gleamed dully in the firelight; their hair was frizzed out wildly, and their noses and ears decorated with ornaments of shell and bone. Back of them, fully armed and accompanying the shrieking of the women by guttural shouts were the warriors.

From time to time one would whirl wildly on one foot, race madly in the direction of the hut where the whites sat, hurl his spear at the hut as he dashed past, then circle until he once more reached his fellows.

Well Blake knew the meaning of that. The savages had excited themselves until they were crazy with the desire for "long pig" (human flesh).

They felt certain the little band of whites were at their mercy, and would keep up the anticipatory dance until the final bestial ceremonies when the spear throwing would give place to a concerted rush. Then the torture, and then the cooking-pot.

It was a desperate situation as it stood, and Blake knew it. He hadn't the slightest doubt but that Black McCabe was responsible for the savages getting out of hand. Yet, as his mind worked madly seeking some plan to put forth to his two companions who sat motionless waiting for the word to move, Blake found, not an added terror in the fact that the savages were cannibals, but a crumb of comfort.

And for this reason, had their sole desire been to overcome the whites and destroy them, it is safe to say that not all the white men could do would hold them off for long.

A burning brand hurled at the grass-plaited hut would soon roast them out, and a dash from the blazing inferno would mean but a dash into a forest of spearheads.

This might suit even the cannibals, but there was the danger that their victims might be destroyed by the fire, and that would mean the loss of their banquet.

Blake was not sorry in a way that his own blacks had deserted him. If their terror should send them fleeing for their own village, Johnson, the trader, would hear what had happened, and might be able to drive a larger force back as a rescue party.

There was but a slender thread of hope in that, but it was at least an added incentive to hold out as long as possible; though when the weary march to the coast was considered it was not very alluring.

So far, Tinker and Captain Weeks had said nothing. They alternately watched the dancing cannibals and their silent leader, waiting for his decision. The option of deciding however, was not to be left to Blake for, while the shrieking fiends still circled the fire, something happened which brought the dance to a sudden end, and precipitated the rush which Blake had anticipated.

The cause of it all was one of the village pigs, and, had not such grave issues hinged on the affair, its ludicrous side would have sent the white men into peals of laughter. As it was, it but deepened the lines of anxiety upon their brows.

It was during the period of the dance just preceding the leaping ceremony of the men, when they would dash through the lines of dancers at full speed, and hurl their spears into a tree which had been set up in the village open space. Then would come a more frenzied performance than ever until, brains dizzied with bestial excitement, they would proceed to the feast.

One or two had even run the gauntlet of the dancers, and had gone whirling madly around the tree when down the human lane dashed something which was not in the performance. It was one of the village pigs which had been started on its career of fright by some unknown cause.

Perhaps the shrieking of the savages had startled it, or perhaps something in the jungle was the cause, but whatever the reason, it raced forward blindly, throwing the ranks of the dancers into confusion.

With cries of rage, the savages gave up the ceremony, and pursued it. The spears which had been meant for the tree were sent whizzing at the pig, and from the moment when the first one struck it an orgy of killing started.

Round and round the village went the pig with the whole band of savages after it. For the moment the whites seemed to have been forgotten. Yet a dash for freedom would have been madness, for once in the open the attention of the savages would be directed towards them, and the animal slaughter which was proceeding would be turned into one with human victims.

Then while the three whites still followed the course of the mad chase, the pig, driven desperate by its multitude of wounds and blinded by its own blood, plunged into the very midst of the big fire.

A startled squeal went up and there immediately followed the smell of scorching flesh. Racing forward, the savages hurled more spears into the beast, and as it dropped dead, they staggered back with distended nostrils.

Their lust for killing had given way to their lust for gorging, and as those odours worked their way into their senses they bethought themselves of the human delicacies which awaited them. All thought of ceremony now fled.

As one man they turned, and, regarded the hut which held their victims; then to the accompaniment of mad shrieks and yells, they raised their spears, and hurled themselves forward. There was only one thing for the three whites to do, and they did it.

Even before the blacks had started, Blake, who scented what was coming, issued his commands:

"Captain Weeks," he said. "You will kneel at the right hand side of the doorway. I will take up my place at the left. Tinker, you will throw yourself flat on the ground between us and fire from that position.

"Don't waste a shot. Every one will count. Pick your man, then let him have it. The more deadly our fire, the quicker we shall cause an impression. Our one hope is to drive them back sufficiently to enable us to make a dash. Now then, ready! Here they come!"

As one man they took up their positions, and held their revolvers ready. The dash was just starting, and already some of the stronger arms were hurling spears. On they came, the firelight throwing their leaping bodies into bold relief, and if it enabled them to see better it also helped the whites to pick their marks.

Yard after yard they covered until the defenders could see their lustful features then, when they began to open out a little, Blake's revolver barked. Like a double echo the other two flashed out, and the three figures which went down with a crash told how well had been the marksmanship of the defenders.

But three out of the thirty or more, who formed the attacking party were not many, and the little band of desperate whites realised every shot must tell if they were to drive the savages back. Again and again they fired into the ranks of the savages and man after man went down.

Yet the hail of spears seemed not to abate a jot, and unless the defenders brought down several more the sweep of the charge would carry the cannibals upon them.

Never before had anyone of them fired more rapidly than at that time. Shot after shot rang out, shell after shell flew to one side as the automatics ejected them, clip after clip was thrust in as the empty ones were withdrawn and tossed to one side.

So far the three defenders had escaped being wounded. Many of the spears had passed uncomfortably close to them, and the shafts of more than one had struck them, but not yet had the savages drawn blood.

On their side, however, the loss had been heavy. Five men lay huddled up where they had fallen, and as many more had dragged themselves away badly wounded. And as the odds against them were decreased so were the chances of the defenders, increased in like proportion.

It was when the oncoming blacks were barely twenty feet away, that Blake's voice again rang out.

"Now then, into their very midst," he cried. "Fire as rapidly as possible."

Even as he spoke his own revolver was barking viciously, and Tinker's tension relieved itself in an exclamation as four more savages went down. Still they kept up that deadly hail of lead, and all three gave vent to a hoarse cheer as the ranks of the enemy parted, and they circled back towards the fire.

The first attack had been repulsed, and so far not one of the defenders had been scratched. But Blake knew the breathing spell would not last long. The savages had again met and were discussing the next move. That many of them favoured the use of burning brands was evident from their gesticulations, and the frequent pointings towards the fire.

It was soon seen, however, that the majority favoured a repetition of the first tactics, and as they once more massed for the charge, Blake turned to his companion.

"They are going to charge again. The moment they get on this side of the big fire, let them have it. If we do much damage be ready to charge when I give the word. Now they are coming. That big one covered with the shell decorations is my man. Fire!"

Their revolvers flashed out as Blake spoke, and how well he had judged his mark could be seen when the savage to which he had referred went sprawling to the ground.

On came the rest of them, however, leaping and screaming more frenziedly than ever, and for some moments, it seemed that their very madness would carry them through the hail of lead which was being poured into them.

But even into their crazed minds was hurled the thought that they were losing heavily. Savages though they were, and uncaring of the fate of their fellows as was their nature, still they realised that over half of their force had been incapacitated, and as far as they knew the three lone whites still remained unharmed.

It must have been borne in upon them that brute force would not overcome that stubborn resistance. Much had they heard of the all-conquering white man, but never before had they met him in combat, and the present disastrous result must have caused them to think as much as their primitive minds could think.

At any rate, they could not but see what the inevitable result must be if they continued to hurl themselves against that shower of lead which met them with such deadly effect. To continue would be but suicide, and would result in the eventual extermination of the whole force of fighting men in the village.

Whatever the reason, the visible results of the prowess of the whites caused them to part once more just before they reached the hut, and this time when they again met behind the big fire, the watchers in the hut could see that not one man negatived the gesticulated suggestions in the direction of the fire.

"They won't rush again," said Blake, watching them keenly. "They have had enough lead, and now they will try what they consider to be strategy. Ah, I thought so! See that one making towards the fire? Do you catch the idea?

"He will take a burning brand and bind it to his spear, then from a safe distance he will hurl it at the hut. A few of those will soon set it ablaze and then we will be smoked out.

"I think that now is our time. We have driven them off twice and they fear us. But if we remain where we are we give them a chance to recover and place ourselves at their mercy.

"Besides, a neighbouring village may turn up at any moment and reinforce them. In my opinion our best chance of safety lies in taking the bull by the horns and rushing them. What do you say?"

"I think we should follow up our advantage as you suggest," grunted the captain. "The black fiends! I never thought I'd enjoy bowling over a nigger as I have to-night."

"And you, Tinker?"

"Same here, guv'nor. Whatever you say goes."

"Then since we are all agreed I think it is best to lose no time. Are you both ready?"

"Ay, ready!" exclaimed the captain and Tinker in one voice.

"Then, follow me. Up! Ready! Charge!"

"With Blake leading the trio dashed out of the hut, revolvers levelled, and sending up a shout that rivalled the war cry of the blacks. In the very act of plucking a burning brand from the fire half a dozen of the savages glanced up, startled, then very hastily gathered up their spears and prepared to meet the daring trio.

What would have been the result of that last desperate struggle had the two parties come together as they were then matched it is hard to say. Perhaps when the final test came the indomitable courage of the whites would have carried them through, or mayhap the spears of the blacks would have levelled them before their bullets had found a billet.

But the result on that basis was never to be known, for, to the unbounded astonishment of both parties, reinforcements suddenly came to the whites. And those reinforcements were none other than the six carriers who had dashed off into the jungle at the first sign of trouble.

Not even Blake realised that it was nothing but his own personality which was responsible for this sudden access of courage on the part of his carriers; but, as a matter of fact, such was the case.

From the security of the jungle they had watched the whole progress of the fight, and when, after those two terrific onslaughts, the little party of whites had dashed out, unscathed, it had raised once more their belief in the magic of the man who had been their master.

The rapidly-dropping blacks had clinched this, and when the trio charged in their turn they had leaped from their place of concealment, and with brandished spears had joined in the fray against their age-old enemies, the hill tribe.

Their appearance was exactly the thing needed to turn the balance in Blake's favour. As they swept across the open the village fighting men stood still poised for fight, then, as their eyes once more encountered the unwavering line of levelled revolvers, they hesitated and were lost. Another moment they stood, then turned, and made off pell-mell into the forest.

An involuntary sigh of relief went up from Blake as they broke and fled, for though the lust of battle had welled up in him as strongly as in his companions, he realised that a temporary victory would give them no real advantage, and that if a neighbouring village should send a force the tables would be soon turned.

Therefore, he welcomed the victory as the opportunity he had been looking for, and, instead of following his natural desire to make chase, he controlled himself and called out a curt command to his own party to do likewise.

Tinker and Captain Weeks stopped at once, contenting themselves by sending a few shots in the direction of the flying savages. But Blake was compelled to send a second and sharper command at the carriers before they gave up.

When they came back he did not make the mistake of thanking them for their timely assistance, but, registering a resolve that he should reward them on reaching the coast, he hauled them over the coals for their desertion. Then he had them gather up what packs remained and prepare for a dash.

He, Tinker, and the captain lost no time in getting together their own things, and it was but a few minutes after the cannibals had disappeared into the jungle on one side of the village when Blake and his party set off hotfoot at the other.

Just as they were starting the head boy of his carriers came to Blake and told him the white man he had been seeking had really been in the village, and that, just as the fight started, they had seen him leave quietly, accompanied by four blacks.

That meant he had taken advantage of the success of the fight he had precipitated to make his escape, and it was with a grim nod that Blake realised what that start might mean to him. Travelling light, and with the mountain blacks to guide him, he must necessarily travel faster than they.

Besides, he had a good four hours' start, and on the long, tortuous trail to the coast could easily turn that into twelve. For the sake of his carriers Blake must go slow, but even though McCabe had the start Blake rested secure in the thought that the renegade had no means of leaving Rubilinga.

At the same time he pushed on as fast as conditions would permit. All night, they travelled steadily, and when morning broke they breathed easier. They had thoroughly expected a running fight with the mountain blacks, but none had shown up, and by noon they should be out of the hill country.

Blake had barely congratulated himself on this when an exclamation from Tinker caused him to turn, and he dashed back as he saw Captain Weeks reeling in his tracks. One look told him what was the matter.

The march, the fight, and the excitement had proved too much for the seaman. He was in the grip of jungle fever and even as Blake reached him he collapsed.

A good two hours were consumed dosing the sick man, rearranging the loads, and dividing the party so that four men could be constantly told off to carry the captain. Blake fixed it so each quartette should carry the captain for an hour, then assume the loads of the others, leaving the sick man for them.

He and Tinker both did their share, and in this fashion they stumbled on through the afternoon, taking turn and turn about, though not for a moment were they free of a load of some sort. Even Pedro carried a bundle of food strapped to his back, and it was a very exhausted party which camped that night.

Ever since the captain had collapsed Blake had given up all hope of keeping Black McCabe's advantage down to twelve hours. He realised now that before they again saw the trading station the renegade would be a good day ahead.

Had he dreamed what was taking place at the station even as they made camp he would have been tempted to have dashed on ahead, single handed. But he did not know, so, like a good leader he gave his party the rest they so sorely needed, and that night it was he and Tinker who kept watch.

The captain was now delirious and, at times, violent. Owing to this the next day's progress was even slower. They stopped at midday for a hasty meal, then on again through the afternoon.

It was past six when the first tang of the sea struck their nostrils, and with the smell came fresh vigour to the little party. The sun was just dropping into the sea like a golden orange when at last they broke out of the jungle into the coconut palms surrounding the station, but even as they did so what a sight revealed itself.

The station was no longer there. The store and the shacks had disappeared. Nothing but a heap of smoking ruins met them. And to add to their consternation the trim schooner by which they had come was no longer in the lagoon.

Blake was squatting by the smouldering embers near
the doorway, keeping watch.

TO understand why Blake's party came upon a smoking and deserted trading station instead of the apparently-prosperous place they had left it is necessary to relate the startling occurrences which had taken place there after the whaleboat had left the lagoon bearing the news of the disaster to the Kara Maru.

When the boat had finally disappeared through the passage leading to the open sea, Johnson, the trader, turned and made his way back to the hut where lay the sole survivor of the wreck. On entering the shack he found that his guest was not only awake but sitting on the edge of the cot apparently much refreshed by the food and sleep.

Never for a moment did it enter the trader's mind to doubt the man who had come to Rubilinga in such a strange fashion. That he had been on the Kara Maru was true enough, and there was no reason for the trader to guess that the name of William Carr, which the other had given, was not his name at all but the name of one of the Yankee sailors who had gone down with the ship.

Nor did he for one second dream that the man before him was a far greater and far more accomplished world-criminal than the criminal who had escaped into the bush, and that, even as he sat there, he had on him one of the most priceless pearls ever taken from the sea.

Yet such was the case, for Rymer it was and no other. His cool daring and magnificent physique had carried him safely through what had seemed certain death, and now, as he realised he had really won out, his fertile brain was already devising plans to get away from Rubilinga with the booty he had gained.

For once in his career Rymer felt that luck had been with him in every way. There he was, the only survivor of the wreck. Anyone who knew about the crimson pearl would at once conclude that it had gone to the bottom of the sea when the ship sank.

The two Chinese who had coveted it had also lost their lives, and did any accomplices of theirs exist, they would think the obvious —that is, that the pearl had gone, too.

It seemed a piece of almost unbelievable good fortune that he had succeeded his snatching a fortune from the jaws of death. And not only that, but, from the garments of the dead Ferguson and his

Celestial murderer, he had gained sufficient funds to enable him to go on for some time without the necessity for recourse to the pearl.

He was a connoisseur in stones, and realised only too well what a stir would be caused by the advent into the market of the crimson pearl. To dispose of it in the ordinary way was out of the question.

He must think up some other plan, but he had not the slightest doubt that some private collector would jump at the chance of acquiring it for a big price.

At any rate, he could now afford to move cautiously, and even as he sat pondering the matter Rymer registered a vow that the strike he had made should keep him in idle luxury for the rest of his days. Therefore, he was in a decidedly hopeful frame of mind when the trader entered the shack.

"I needn't ask you if you feel better," said Johnson cheerily. "I can see that. You have had a pretty tough experience, Carr."

Rymer nodded;

"Yes. I never want to go through it again. Thanks to you, I am almost as well as ever now. By the way, what are the chances of getting away from here?"

The trader smiled.

"I am afraid you will have to content yourself here for a few days at least. The schooner in the lagoon will be leaving then, and I have no doubt but that they will land you at some port or other."

"Then she doesn't belong to you?"

"No. She is chartered to a gentleman who has gone into the bush, I expect him back most any time now. My own schooner won't be here for another fortnight yet. She is fitting out at Port Moresby."

"I don't suppose you have anything else by which I could get away? I think I should report the disaster to the owners as soon as possible."

"There is no need for worry on that score; I have already sent the news."

"How do you mean?"

"The only boat I had which could make a sea journey was a big whaleboat. One of the sailors who rescued you took charge of her, and with a crew of natives set off less than an hour ago for an island sixty miles away, where there is a wireless station. They should reach there this evening, and by to-night the world will know of the loss of the Kara Maru. I —Why, what is the matter?"

The trader broke off, and uttered the exclamation as he saw the sudden change of expression which swept over Rymer's face. It was but a momentary unveiling of the true man behind that bearded mask, and, though it lasted but a second, a chill went down Johnson's back as he saw the flickering devil of rage in the other's eyes.

In a moment, however, it had gone, but the forced laugh which followed it did not sweep away the feeling which had run over the trader.

"Nothing —nothing at all," answered Rymer. "It was a twinge of pain. Er —you say the whaleboat has already gone?"

"Yes; less than an hour."

"I am sorry. I should have been glad to go by her. And there is no other chance before the schooner leaves?"

"None."

"This gentleman who has her chartered and has gone into the bush —you think he will return shortly?"

"As I told you, I expect him any day. He has gone in on a special mission."

"Then I suppose I must content myself until he returns," said Rymer, with another forced smile.

"That is all you can do. I will send a black boy to look after your wants, and if you feel in the need of company come over to the store. I am usually there."

With that, the trader nodded, and turned to leave. But as he made his way towards his own shack he muttered:

"Scott! He is a strange fellow. I didn't like that look on his face when I told him the whaleboat had gone. Now, I wonder why he was so upset on hearing that? I should think he would be glad of the rest. I'll guarantee he would be an ugly customer if he were crossed. But ugly or not, he will have to kick his heels here until the schooner leaves."

And back in the shack Rymer was sitting cursing with all his strength. He could have throttled the trader when he heard the whaleboat had gone, but with his feeling of rage had come the thought that he could only lose by showing his hand, so he had controlled himself.

But he had no fancy for going by the schooner, where he would of necessity be subjected to many awkward questions. His own desire was to avoid publicity, for therein lay safety. Yet there seemed nothing for it but to content himself until the schooner should leave, so he made up his mind to do so.

For the rest of that day he was busy going through the money and papers he had taken from the clothes of Ferguson and the Chinaman. He found that the latter contained nothing of any value to him excepting the information from some of Ferguson's that the value of the crimson pearl was fully recognised by its owners, and that it was intended for Lord Cambrey.

This also put him in possession of the truth regarding Ferguson's journey, and the reason he had been followed by the two Celestials. He smiled grimly as he thought of the fate of his two rivals, and lovingly toyed with the pearl as he arranged it securely around his neck.

He burnt all the papers after reading them, and although it hurt him to destroy the drafts which Ferguson had carried, he realised they were of no use to him. As soon as it was known that the Kara Mara had gone down payment on them would be stopped.

Then for two long days he was forced to sit about doing nothing. He found little pleasure in talking to the trader, and ever since their last interview in the shack Johnson had left Rymer alone.

He greeted him pleasantly enough when he came to the store, but he had not forgotten the momentary unveiling of his guest's rage, and from that moment had been filled with mistrust of him.

On the evening of the second day Rymer became strangely restless. A fever of impatience was consuming him, and when he looked at the idle schooner out in the lagoon his control was in danger of breaking bounds. Not yet was there any sign of the party which had gone into the bush, and rather than acknowledge further his anxiety to depart Rymer forbore questioning the trader.

After his evening meal of rice and bananas, he retired to his shack early and lay down on the cot to think. The restless spirit which consumed him, however, would not leave him in peace, so, after a few moments, he stumbled to his feet and began pacing up and down the narrow confines of the shack.

Outside, the night was still and close. There had not been a breath of wind all day, and the sinking of the sun had brought no relief from the humid heat of the day. In a spirit of irritation, Rymer again threw himself down, then in a moment he was up once more.

"The trouble with me is the heat," he muttered. "I'll drag the cot over by the door, and see if that helps any. Heavens, but I'll be glad to get out of here!"

As he grunted his protest at the forced delay to his plans he jerked the cot away from the wall, and pulled it across until it was close to the low open door of the shack. Then he turned to extinguish the candle, but as he did so stopped, with a sudden look of puzzlement.

Now, the floor of the shack was of mud, beaten hard by much use. So far Rymer had seen no sign of a break in it. Its surface had been as unbroken as though it were of cement, but as he stood gazing at the spot where the cot had stood he saw that the hard-packed surface had been broken and turned up.

A distinct mound rose just under where the middle of the cot had been, and a natural curiosity to know why filled Rymer. He stepped quickly towards it, and, reaching for a small axe near at hand, began turning over the loose soil.

He had been working for the space of perhaps five minutes, and had succeeded in uncovering a fair-sized hole, when a slight noise at the door caused him to turn sharply.

As he did so he found himself gazing into the mouth of a heavy revolver, and at the same moment the man behind it spoke.

"Put up your hands. If you make a move, I will fill you full of lead."

Rymer did not attempt to disobey. He was wise enough to realise the other had the drop on him, and in the tones had been a determined meaning. At first he thought it must be Johnson, the trader, for the words had been English, but as his eyes made out the dark features behind the revolver he saw, to his surprise, that it was a stranger.

At once came the thought that it must be a member of the expedition which had gone into the jungle. Whoever it was Rymer decided that he should make the next move.

Nor was he kept waiting long, for almost at once the stranger spoke again.

"Who are you, and what are you doing here?" he demanded, advancing a step into the shack.

"If the information will be of any particular interest to you I don't mind telling you," responded Rymer coolly. "I was shipwrecked here four days ago."

"Has there been a shipwreck here? Mind, if you lie to me, I'll shoot you as I would a dog."

"I told you there had been, and I meant it. You can't frighten me, my friend. If you think it will pay you to shoot, go ahead."

"What kind of a ship was wrecked, and how many survivors were there?"

"A big passenger steamer was wrecked —the Kara Maru, bound from Brisbane to Hong Kong. I was the only survivor."

As Rymer finished speaking, the other took several steps forward and bent to scrutinise him closely. As he did so the light from the candle fell full on his face, and after one single glance of utter amazement, Rymer deliberately lowered his arms and smiled.

"Well, if it isn't my old friend, Black McCabe!" he said softly. "What is the noted London criminal doing in the South Sea Islands?"

With a snarl, the other jerked up his head, and for a moment his finger hovered on the trigger.

"By heavens, who are you?" he snapped. "If you are a 'tec, you had better say your prayers quick."

"Not so fast, Black," said Rymer coolly. "You are growing nervous in your old age. I am no 'tec. Don't you remember me?"

McCabe bent forward again and looked into Rymer's eyes. Then he straightened up, and amazement was pictured on his features as he did so.

"It isn't —it can't be Rymer, the king crook," he muttered half-dazedly.

Rymer smiled again.

"Right first time, Black. So you remember me, eh! Let me see, it is nearly two years since we brought off that little job in Paris, isn't it? And since then you have pulled off a big coup in London, and stirred up the police of every country for your pains. You see, I keep up with events. But what are you doing in this forsaken hole?"

Black McCabe thrust his revolver into his pocket, and looked warily about him. Then he bent close and whispered:

"I was hounded here, and thought I was safe at last. But four days ago, whom do you think arrived in a schooner?"

"Whom?"

"Sexton Blake."

Rymer almost leaped into the air as the name dropped from McCabe's lips. His hand shot out and caught the lesser crook in a grip of steel.

"Say that again!" he demanded excitedly. "Do you mean Sexton Blake is the man who has that schooner chartered?"

"None other, I tell you. He landed here four days ago on my trail, after following me over halfway round the world. I took to the bush, but the cursed trader here betrayed me. Blake made up a party and followed. But for once he bit off more than he could chew. He will never come out of the jungle alive."

"Why not?"

"Because when I started back he was surrounded by a bunch of cannibals who meant mischief. I told them Blake was there to give them the evil eye, and it did the trick. By now he will have gone under. They were beginning the attack when I left."

"I wouldn't be too sure of that," answered Rymer curtly. "I have seen him in pretty tight positions, but he always escaped from them. Heavens, if I had only known that before! But now that you are back here what do you propose doing, Black?"

"The first thing I intend to do is to shoot that traitorous trader," snarled McCabe. "I told him if he gave me away I would kill him — and, by heavens, I intend to do it!"

"And then?"

"Get away somehow. What are you doing here, Rymer? And was that yarn about the shipwreck a straight one?"

"The solemn truth; I had intended waiting here until the people who had the schooner came back, then I was going to leave with them. But I didn't dream that it was Sexton Blake. He may or may not come back, but in any event my plans must be changed. I say, Black, you want to get away from here, don't you?"

"I want to and I am going to."

"Then why not join forces? Our interests are the same, and together we may work the thing with more success. What do you say?"

"I'd like to hitch up with you again, Rymer, but only on one condition."

"What is that?"

"That there is no sharing up with any haul I have made lately."

"My dear fellow, I don't want anything of yours. I am on Easy Street myself. Is that why you pulled a gun on me? Have you buried your London swag under the floor here?"

McCabe nodded.

"Yes, I couldn't take it into the bush with me, so buried it. But if we are going to figure out some scheme to get out of this hole we had better get busy."

"True enough, but first I would suggest that you give up your thoughts of vengeance on the trader. To kill him is not going to do you any good and will only add to the desire of the law to catch you. London is foaming over that last affair."

"Perhaps you are right, Rymer. Anyway, I'll see. Now what do you suggest? I have four of the hill blacks concealed in the bush. We can count on them if necessary."

"I have discovered that at present there is only one way to leave this island," said Rymer slowly. "That way is by the schooner in the lagoon. If the party to which she belongs returns it is safe to bet that we will leave by her, Black, but not as passengers. We will be consigned to the hold and probably kept in irons until we are handed over to the authorities in Port Moresby or Thursday Island.

"I have discovered further that there is now only one white sailor and four Kanakas on board. The other sailor left two days ago for another island to take the news of the wreck. Now isn't it clear to you what I am driving at?"

"You mean?"

"That we capture the schooner and force the Kanakas to work her."

Rymer had succeeded in uncovering a fair-sized hole, when a noise caused him to turn sharply.

The seaman swung round, to find himself gazing into the mouth
of Rymer's revolver.

THE SIXTH CHAPTER.   *Tricked —The Escape.*

FOR a full minute Black McCabe looked at Rymer in silent admiration. Then he spoke.

"By Heavens, Rymer! I believe you have hit it. Exactly what do you propose?"

"In doing whatever we decide upon we must consider several things," answered the king crook slowly. "First, we must not build too firmly on the supposition that Blake and his party will never return from the jungle.

"If you had had the experience of that gentleman that I have had you would realise just how slippery he is. He seems blessed —or cursed —with more lives than a cat, but believe me, Black, if I hadn't something more important on I would like nothing better than to remain here and assist at Sexton Blake's funeral.

"However, my present game is to keep clear of him, and I propose doing so. I am not going to risk running my head into a noose merely to give him his congé. I tried that more than once, and the result was I lost.

"I have rarely played for a bigger stake than at present, and, since it now holds practically no risk in it, I am not going to spoil it. That is my chief reason for insisting that whatever move we make we make it without delay.

"The next thing to consider is the schooner itself. Now, while I have been here, I have had little to do but look around, and that has given me an opportunity to get acquainted with her and the habits of her crew.

"At present she is in charge of the white sailor and four Kanakas, but the man who took the news of the wreck to the island where the wireless is situated should be back at any time. In fact, he was expected yesterday.

"The island is only sixty miles away, and both wind and sea have been favourable for his return. He may have been detained for half a dozen different reasons. They don't concern us, but the date of his return does. To-night we have one white and four Kanakas to reckon with. To-morrow we may have another white man.

"Now, my idea is this —that we move to-night. We can make our way down to the beach and take one of the canoes. By it we can reach the schooner, and before the purpose of our visit is guessed, we can capture her.

"I know Kanakas and how to handle them. I also know the way out of the lagoon, and once at sea we will be safe. Then ho! for Thursday Island. What do you say?"

"If we can work it, it will be bully," responded McCabe. "How about the trader?"

"We will endeavour to get possession of the schooner without rousing his suspicions. Once on board it won't make any difference."

"Right-ho, Rymer! I am with you. How soon do we start?"

"At once. Get your swag together. It ought not to take you long, considering the size of the hole I have made already."

Black McCabe's dark, evil face broke into what was intended to be a smile at Rymer's pleasantry.

"It is a good thing I did not shoot on sight, as I intended," he answered. "I could not imagine who it was."

He crossed to the heap of dirt which Rymer had turned up, and with his bare hands began scratching away at the bottom of the hole. Rymer sat and smoked leisurely while his accomplice worked, and when a grunt of satisfaction escaped the latter he hardly turned his eyes.

"Struck it?" he asked laconically.

"Yes."

In proof of his words McCabe straightened up with a heavy canvas bag in his hands. This he laid to one side, then bent over the hole again. Two more he brought to light before he finished, and squatting beside them, he looked more like a swarthy vulture guarding its prey than the human being he was. Such is the degenerating result of evil and depravity.

He was about to speak again when a faint sound in the direction of the door caused both him and Rymer to swing sharply. Just as they did so they were greeted by the curt tones of Johnson, the trader, and as the voice was backed up by a heavy revolver and determined eyes their hands went up in response to his command.

"Now you two beauties," went on the trader, when they had complied. "I have been listening to your little plot. I know you, McCabe, for what you are, and if your boast that you have set the hill tribes on Sexton Blake's party is true, you will get all that is due to you.

"I suppose these bags on the floor hold the stuff you got in London after shooting the watchman of the bank. That little job will come pretty near to costing you your life, I'm thinking.

"As for you, Mr. William Carr, alias Rymer, it happens that I know a little something about you as well. Such things as newspapers come even to Rubilinga, but I never thought I should have the pleasure of entertaining two such choice scoundrels as you two.

"So you would try to hoodwink me and seize the schooner, eh? Well, luckily I overheard you and have been able to nip that little scheme in the bud.

"Instead of sailing away as lords of her, you will go in the hold, and, believe me, the irons will be strong enough to prevent you from playing any more of your little games until you are handed over to the proper authorities.

"Now then, up with you both and march. By Heavens, if either of you attempt any funny business I will shoot without a second's hesitation. Do you get me?"

Rymer, who had not moved an eyelash all the time the trader had been speaking, smiled slowly, and exchanged a quick glance with McCabe. What the latter read in it it is hard to say, but there seemed no doubt in his mind what he was to do, for, while Rymer turned back to Johnson, McCabe's right arm began to relax ever so gently.

"It isn't hard to follow what you say," said Rymer, eyeing the trader and compelling his gaze in return. "The only point worthy of discussion is that you seem to have hold of the wrong end of the stick. You appear to be under the impression that we are two well-known criminals?"

The trader snorted. So worked up was he that he did not guess for a moment that Rymer was merely sparring for time and to keep his attention.

"I know what I know," he snapped. "If there is any room for doubt you will have an opportunity of explaining it to the judge and jury."

"You hold out an attractive prospect, my friend," smiled Rymer. "I suppose you feel quite certain in your own mind that the programme you have arranged will be carried out."

"I certainly do, and, moreover, we have had enough talk. Get ready! I am going to put you two where you will be safe."

"Since you have the drop on us there seems to be nothing else to do. Now, Black! Quick!" Rymer broke off, and cried out to McCabe as, out of the corner of his eye, he saw that his accomplice was ready to act. Realising at once that he was in danger of losing his advantage, the trader turned sharply, and even as he swung pulled the trigger.

The bullet whistled past McCabe's head, but almost before it had gone plunging through the grass-plaited wall of the shack, the criminal had jerked out his own revolver and sent two shots at the trader.

The first caught Johnson in the shoulder and sent him staggering, just as he pulled the trigger of his own gun the second time. Like his first shot the second went wide, but McCabe's did not. It came plunging across the hut, cut a deep furrow along Johnson's left arm, glanced off and buried itself in his heart just as Rymer leaped forward.

"You fool," he snarled at McCabe. "Why did you shoot to kill. It wasn't the thing to do. Haven't you enough on your hands now?"

"It was a fair fight," replied the other doggedly. "He fired first."

"Can you make any jury believe that? I meant you to put him out of business for the time being. Now the whole station will be roused and we shall have our work cut out to do as we planned.

"Anyway, it can't be helped now. Gather up that swag of yours and come on. Our only hope is in reaching the schooner before the place discovers what has happened."

As he spoke Rymer was already gathering up his own few belongings. McCabe followed suit, rapidly stuffing the heavy canvas bags in his pockets. Then with drawn revolvers and Rymer in the lead, they leaped over the body of the dead trader and started for the beach.

Even as they ran they could see that the sound of firing had roused the station. Lights were already showing in several shacks in the native quarters, and up at the spot where the trader lived, all was commotion. One or two blacks appeared as they ran on, but these the two crooks disregarded.

The whole success of their plan now hinged on gaining schooner. As they reached the coconut grove and plunged into its darkness a shout went up behind them, followed by a pandemonium of cries. It was only too evident that some of the blacks had stumbled upon Johnson's body.

"Hurry up!" panted Rymer. "In five minutes the whole place will be in a turmoil."

"I don't fear the blacks much," jerked McCabe. "I controlled them by hypnotism before and probably could again."

"Hypnotism won't be much good if they run amok," snapped Rymer. "Ah! There is the beach at last. Make to the right. There are half a dozen canoes pulled up over there."

They changed their course a trifle as they struck the top line of the beach and stumbled on across the sand. To their ears now came more distinctly than ever the shouts and cries behind them, for their feet made no sound in the soft sand.

Another hundred yards and Rymer pulled up beside a rough native canoe.

"This one will do, Black. Now listen. This is the best yarn for us to tell when we get to the schooner. When we get within hail we will call out and say the blacks have risen and have wounded the trader.

"The sailor on board knows about you, but has no suspicion of me, so I will do the talking. I will tell him that you are the trader and are too badly hurt to talk. You keep in the shadow and he won't spot you.

"Then, when we get close, I will go aboard first and cover him. You can follow at once, and between us we can control the Kanakas. Do you understand?"

"Sure! I'm ready!"

"Then hop in and I will push off. Don't forget —be low in the boat."

With an understanding nod McCabe climbed in and ensconced himself amidships. Rymer then pushed off, and, leaping over the gunwale, made his way to the stern. Squatting there he took a paddle and with deft strokes set the canoe heading for the schooner.

Evidently the shots and yells at the station had roused the solitary white man on board, for as they neared the schooner, a strong cockney voice floated over the purple waters of the lagoon.

"Boat ahoy! What is the matter?"

Rymer lifted his paddle and let the canoe run ahead of her own accord.

"Blacks have risen," he shouted. "Johnson has been wounded. This is Carr, shipwrecked seaman talking. I am bringing Johnson out here for safety."

"Right-ho! Come alongside, and I will give you a hand up."

Again Rymer's paddle sent streaks of brilliant phosphorescence dancing about as it took the water, and when the canoe got still closer to the schooner, they could see the unsuspecting sailor leaning over the side ready to assist them.

"Is he badly hurt?" he called.

"Pretty bad," answered Rymer. "All ready, heave your rope. Good! I have it. Now wait until I fasten it on Johnson, then I will come up and lend a hand."

He bent over the huddled form of Black McCabe as he spoke, and made a pretence of fastening the rope about the other's shoulders.

"When I call, Black, come up," he whispered.

McCabe nodded, and straightening himself, Rymer looked up at the shadowy figure of the seaman.

"I guess the rope will hold all right. I'm coming up now."

"Right-ho! my hearty. Come along."

Rymer grasped the rope, and as expertly as the dead William Carr whose name he had stolen could have done it, he swarmed up. On reaching the deck, he dropped beside the sailor, and turned as though to help him hoist the man in the canoe.

Instead, however, his hand went to his pocket, and when the seaman swung to ask if Rymer were ready, he found himself gazing into the mouth of the latter's revolver. One single word did Rymer utter. That word was "Black."

In response to it, McCabe came up hand over hand, and to the astonishment of the sailor, dropped easily to the deck.

"Why, why what is this?" he stuttered. "I thought —"

"Never mind what you thought," interrupted Rymer quietly. "This is the thought you want to get fixed in your mind. If you make a move, or cry out, I shall pull this trigger, and let me tell you it works very easily. Now, then, Black, take some of that rope off the deck, and truss him up. I don't see the Kanakas, but they are liable to show up on deck at any moment. Hurry up."

"By thunder, you will suffer for this," blazed the sailor. "What your game is I don't know, but when the captain comes back, you will pay."

"Shut up!" commanded Rymer curtly. "Hurry up, Black. If he opens his mouth again, stuff something into it."

Glowering, the sailor subsided, while McCabe with many deft twists of the rope bound him. The situation was utterly beyond the seaman, and while he was in ignorance of the reason for the piracy of the two before him, he deemed discretion the better part of valour. And therein he was wise, for though Rymer never killed wantonly, he was not the man to stand idle while his plans were delayed.

When McCabe had trussed the sailor up to his satisfaction, he stuffed an old handkerchief into his mouth, and secured it with another. Then, at Rymer's direction, he dragged him across to the open hatch and unceremoniously dropped him through. There was a crash, a groan, then silence.

At the same moment the patter of bare feet sounded up forward, and the two pirates turned to see the four Kanakas running aft. Not till they got past amidships did Rymer speak, but when he did, his voice caused the blacks to bring up short.

A master of the pidgin English used amongst the islands, and thoroughly conversant with the ways of the half civilized men before him, Rymer knew exactly how to handle the present situation.

He made no attempt at explaining the presence of himself and McCabe, and the disappearance of the seaman. Instead he went straight to the crux of the matter.

"You boys get ready, get out long boat," he ordered curtly. "Other man gon long-way. Bush boys rise now. Murder, kill, steal, eat 'long pig.' Kill you, too. Quick move. Pull schooner out."

For a moment they gazed at him in silence, then as though the fates were working for Rymer, a great blase of light shot up behind the coconut palms. Even from the deck of the schooner could be seen the wildly dancing figures of the savages as they whirled madly about the store.

Rymer had spoken truer than he thought. The station was abaze, and the blacks were running amok in grim reality. One long look the four Kanakas took at the scene, then without a word, they turned and raced aft to lower the long boat.

A few minutes later, it took the water with a splash, and under Rymer's direction they pulled it round to the bow. While he arranged a tow rope, McCabe took a knife, and sawed through the anchor ropes.

Freed from that restraint, the schooner began to drift gently towards the shore, but the Kanakas were now pulling, and as the tow rope grew taut, the schooner slowly answered to the pull. Hurrying aft, Rymer took the wheel, and sent McCabe into the bow to urge on the Kanakas.

As the long boat headed for the lagoon passage, and the slim schooner trailed slowly after Rymer heaved a sigh of relief. But he was congratulating himself too soon. Something had impelled the blacks on shore to turn their attention to the lagoon.

To see what was going on was easy now, for the rioters had fired the whole station. It lit up the face of the lagoon like day, and in the midst of the blazing village could be seen the dancing savages, looting and drinking with all the lack of restraint which their wild natures were capable of.

It was more than obvious that blood-lust would have them in its power soon, and even Rymer shuddered as he thought of the scene which would follow. With the trader's death, the last restraint had been withdrawn.

Before the orgy of looting and drinking started, a strong white man might have controlled them, but now that they had started, they would continue until the restraint of months had broken bounds to satiation.

What had started them in the first place it is hard to say, but the probabilities are that the cause lay in the flight of the two white men. On discovering Johnson's body and seeing the flight they would at once conclude that there had been trouble between the whites. That would be sufficient in itself, but the added fact that two of the whites were attempting to leave the island would give additional temptation to them.

At any rate, they were going mad with the effect of the spirits they had found, and even as the schooner started to move Rymer could see them racing for the beach. He shouted to McCabe telling him what was taking place, and urging him to hasten the Kanakas still more.

They, poor creatures, needed no urging. They could see for themselves what was threatening, and well knew what their fate would be did they fall into the hands of the maddened cannibals. They pulled with the strength of twice their number, and in response the schooner slowly accelerated her speed.

That the schooner was moving was now evident to the savages on shore, and their shouts of rage reached Rymer's ears as they ran their canoes into the water. The passage from the lagoon was still a long distance off, and, measuring the chances with a careful eye, Rymer saw that the blacks must overtake them before they could possibly make it.

He called to McCabe to come and take the wheel, then he himself went forward. A few curt words he called to the Kanakas, threatening to shoot them if they attempted to cut the tow rope and escape. After he had made his intention plain, and had assured them that he could hold off the pursuers, he saw to the loading of his revolver, and took up his stand.

"You stick to the wheel, Black," he called. "Don't leave it until I say. If I can't hold them off, and they attempt to board, I will call you. They seem to be carrying spears. As soon as they get within range, I will fire.

"But wait, Black. I have an idea. I am going below for a few moments. Call out if they get very close."

Without waiting for the other to answer, Rymer dashed down the companion-way, and made his way into the small main saloon. He dug about there until he found what he was after —a kerosene tin.

It was nearly half full, and as he saw this, he grunted with satisfaction. Lifting it in his arms, he raced back to the deck with it. There he set it down and leaped forward.

He had previously noticed a great rope net near the forward hatch —one of those netted slings for handling cargo —and as his fertile brain had sought for some plan to overcome his pursuers he had thought of it.

He dragged it along the deck until he reached a small boat which hung from the port davits. Dropping the net, he released the falls, and let the boat drop to the water. Then he pulled and tugged until he got the great net over the side.

It dropped with a thud into the small boat almost capsizing it, but though it listed dangerously, it floated, and when Rymer had lowered himself into it, he shifted the weight of the net, causing the boat to right itself.

Then he worked feverishly. First he unrolled the net, and threw it completely over the boat. After that he dragged four cork fenders from the side of the schooner, and tied one each to a corner of the net. Then he threw each fender as far out as he could, letting the net run after it.

When he had finished, the result was a small boat covered by a rope net which floated out on each side as well as out from the bow and stern for fully twenty feet each way.

Though most of the net was under water, the cork fenders acting as buoys kept it near the surface, and in reality satisfying Rymer better than if it floated on the surface, for now it was practically invisible.

His next move was to tie the middle of the net to one of the seats, and that done he pulled himself up on deck. Snatching up the tin of oil he lowered it into the boat, then he turned to survey the chase.

The blacks were coming up hand over hand, and though the passage from the lagoon was now not far away, the savages must overtake them before they could make it. That was a certainty.

Their shouts and cries reached the schooner audibly, and McCabe's fearful glances behind proved how they affected him. Rymer glanced at him contemptuously.

"He can shoot if he thinks he is safe," he muttered as he made his way forward. "But when it comes to real danger he shows what he is really made of. Now to jog up the Kanakas, then to see how my trap works."

He leaned over the bow, and spoke sharply to the Kanakas, urging them not to slacken their efforts and promising them he would take care of their pursuers. Satisfied that their very fear would make them stick to their labour, he went back along the deck.

One more look he took at the oncoming canoes before going over the side. There were five in all, and each one contained eight or nine blacks. That meant two score to reckon with, but if they held their present close formation, Rymer hoped for success in his strategy.

Still they gained, and when scarcely fifty feet separated them from the schooner, Rymer acted. Dropping into the boat he released it from the falls, and clinging to a rope, which had been fastened to the mainmast, he let the boat run past the schooner until it reached the stern.

There he held it, and looking upwards, called to the puzzled McCabe.

"Be ready to give me a hand up if I need it."

"What are you doing, Rymer?" asked the other leaning over.

"You will see in a moment. Keep the schooner's head for the passage, and leave these fellows to me. Ah! I thought so. They are getting impatient. They are throwing their spears already, but they are not close enough yet to do any damage."

Another minute passed during which the canoes kept up their steady gain, then, when the first spear grazed the stern of the schooner, Rymer acted.

Coolly he bent, and emptied the tin of kerosene into the boat, saturating the whole interior from bow to stern. That done he caught hold of the oil-saturated painter of the boat, and with it in one hand, began drawing himself up to the deck by the other rope.

Reaching there he turned, and gazed at the pursuing canoes. A moment, only he did so, then when he judged them to be about right for his purpose, he calmly lit a match, and touched it to the painter.

For a second there was visible a twisting snake of flame as the oil caught and ran along the rope, which Rymer had immediately tossed back into the small boat. A second only, then a terrific burst of flame, as the oil-soaked boat caught fire from end to end.

The blast of heat struck hard against the faces of the two men in the stern before the schooner had drawn away, then they watched with anxious eyes while it drifted back into the very midst of the five pursuing canoes.

A shout of fear went up from the blacks as they saw the blazing mass which was coming towards them, and those who held the paddles made frantic efforts to get out of the way.

But Rymer had judged well, and exactly what he had anticipated occurred. The savages were able to steer clear of the blazing boat, and, under ordinary circumstances, would have escaped unharmed, but —and that was where Rymer's subtle brain proved itself —they knew nothing of the net which stretched out on every side.

Their paddles went straight into it, and before they could be withdrawn, the impetus of the canoes had carried them forward. In less than a minute the astounded blacks were caught, and there followed a shrieking, burning, tangled pandemonium of maddened savages, beside which their previous yells were like a summer zephyr.

Man after man rose, and attempted to escape by diving over the side. Some succeeded, but the vast majority only got tangled in the net, and in their struggles to free themselves, only made matters worse.

Then the fire swept across the canoes, the whole flotilla blazed up, and even the two hardened men who watched from the stern of the schooner turned away from the spectacle which followed.

There was no need now to prepare to repel boarders. What few blacks had escaped unharmed from that blazing holocaust had been suddenly sobered. They were already swimming for the shore, and as he looked at Rymer, Black McCabe's eyes were filled with admiration.

As for Rymer, he was already on his way to the bow, in order to keep his eye on the Kanakas while they pulled through the passage. Another five minutes brought them to its mouth, and in six its palm-lined coral walls had taken the schooner into their shadow.

Racing back to the stern, Rymer took the wheel from McCabe, sending the latter forward. Slowly, but surely, they slid along through the inky waters, until at last they emerged into the line of flying surf.

At the same moment a faint breath of wind struck them, and, shouting to McCabe, Rymer bade him hoist the jibsail. No sooner had it been loosened out than the wind caught it, and with sufficient way to drive her free of the coral reef, the schooner heeled and nosed the outer waters.

Their work over, the Kanakas let the long boat drift back, and as the schooner passed them, caught the rope which Rymer threw over. They came over the side one after the other, and, letting the long boat run back to the stern, hoisted it up.

This done, they turned to and hauled up the other sails. The schooner was steadily drawing away from the lee of the island, and now, with all sails up, caught the full benefit of the ever-growing breeze.

Steadily she forged ahead, until, when the full strength of the breeze caught her, she heeled over gracefully, and shot forward at a spanking pace, the South Pacific lapping musically at her sides, and the fugitives aboard her staring ahead with hopeful eyes.

DR. HUXTON RYMER.

THOUGH it was obvious to Blake that something of a terrible nature had occurred at the trading station since he and his party had plunged into the bush on their fruitless and all but fatal expedition, he little dreamed exactly how disastrous the situation was. As he shaded his eyes from the setting sun, and gazed across the smouldering heaps which marked where the station had stood, he vainly endeavoured to discern some signs of human life. Not even a village pig was to be seen, and in the Solomon Islands when that village accessory is missing, a place is indeed deserted.

His six black carriers were quite as dumbfounded at the sight as was he. On seeing the ruins, which stretched away to the coconut grove fringing the lagoon, they dropped their burdens and pressed forward. With their rising excitement, the necessity for rigid discipline was borne in upon Blake, and he turned to them sternly.

"Pick up your burdens!" he ordered. "Fall into line! Come, Tinker, up with the captain again. Something serious has happened, and the schooner seems to have departed. If it is anything to do with the blacks we must move warily, and not relax discipline for a moment. All ready, forward!"

Dominated by Blake's cool manner, the carriers obeyed him, and, with the same formation they had held in the jungle, the little party broke cover, and started across the spot which had been the location of the trading station.

Still no human being, black or white, was to be seen; but as they moved along, Blake's keen eyes saw many things which roused a great uneasiness in his breast. There were remains of fires which had no connection with the smoking heaps where had stood the buildings.

There were broken axe handles, and shreds of once gaily-coloured trade cotton, now wet and mud-stained. There were scattered heaps of bones, and many, many dirty strips of pig-hide lying about. A medley of cheap hardware was to be seen in every direction, and more than one empty cask showed what had become of the trader's private stock of spirits.

From end to end of the village were these remains to be seen, and from end to end it spelled one word to Blake, and that word was —loot.

Only too well could he picture the scene which must have taken place while he was in the jungle. The remains were sufficient to enable him to reconstruct it more or less accurately, but the question which kept thundering in his mind was — Why?

What had become of the trader? Where were the blacks, and what had caused them to break out? Had Johnson fallen a victim to their murderous outbreak, or had he escaped by the schooner?

It seemed more reasonable to suppose the latter. Otherwise, what had become of the ship? Yet it did not seem in keeping with the trader's nature, as Blake had judged it, that Johnson would run away and let Blake's party risk a return to the station while it was in the hands of the blacks. Again, where was Black McCabe? It was safe to assume that he had reached the station by the previous evening. Had he arrived whilst the blacks were running amok, and, if so, had he fallen a victim to them? Or had his old hypnotic power over them carried him through? If so, where was he?

Had he any connection with the disappearance of the schooner? In their great need for safety, had he and the trader temporarily joined forces? If the trader were on the schooner, it was pretty certain that he would be beating about not far from the land, if he thought Blake would turn up.

But —and here it was that Blake's uneasiness increased —Black McCabe may have convinced him that Blake's party had been annihilated by the hill tribes, causing the trader to sail away.

If so, it left Blake and those with him in a very precarious position, and none realised it better than the stern-faced man who stood gazing at the ruins, and pondering on this new phase which had arisen.

These and a dozen other questions raced through his mind as he puzzled over the situation. It was evident that what they had seen of the remains of the other blacks' orgy had excited the carriers tremendously, and had it not been for the domination of Blake's personality they would have broken and run long since.

Now, Blake was fully aware that one quality which is almost totally lacking in the Solomon Islander is a sense of gratitude. He was also aware that the foreman of the carriers had begun to look up to him with a doglike devotion, but, at the same time, he did not make the mistake of building too much on the black's loyalty to him.

He knew what the call of the blood meant, and if the black once got the grip of the mad return to nature which had seized his fellows, Blake knew all his influence would be submerged in the greater lust of the flesh. So he reasoned, and therein showed how well he had studied the savage.

But no matter what had happened, one thing was certain. They must make camp, and secure a position of temporary safety before they did anything else. The captain was still delirious, and, consequently, still a burden on them.

Not that Blake minded that, for he had grown immensely fond of the bluff old sea-dog who in the most trying moments had ever had a quip and a jest to lighten the march.

Moreover, it was while in Blake's service that he had gone down, and that but added to the solicitousness which Blake and Tinker felt. It was obvious that the drugs he had anticipated getting on his arrival at the station could not now be procured, so the need for a safe camp was twofold. Captain Weeks must have rest and quiet.

Inwardly Blake was full of foreboding, but outwardly he was the same cool, indomitable leader as he turned to the head black boy, who in Rubilinean dialect, was known as Abonga—"the heavy one."

"Abonga," he said curtly, "we make camp. Hurry!"

The black obediently turned to his fellows, and passed on the order. Then he himself threw down his burden, and got busy. The spot at which Blake had stopped, and where he had chosen to pitch camp, was a spot midway between the mound where the store had stood and the coconut grove.

From it he could command a view of the whole of the ruins as well as the lagoon, and should trouble break out, it left a free run towards the jungle.

He had no doubt but that the blacks had taken to the bush after the orgy, and at that very moment might be either sleeping off the effects, or watching them from the shelter of the distant trees.

He did not know, however, that over half of the pick of the village fighting men had been killed in the attack on the schooner and that, bloodthirsty though the remainder were, they would think twice before they bucked up against the whites again.

In fact, Blake did not even know of the attack in the lagoon. He was in utter ignorance of all that had happened, and could only judge by what he saw.

When camp had been pitched, and a rough shack made of loose material which they found lying about, had been erected, they carried the captain into its shelter, and made him comfortable on a couch of leaves and grass.

Both Tinker and Blake had entered the shack, and while they were busy with the captain, did not see what was happening outside. But on emerging to see after the evening meal, they realised only too well what had occurred. At first, not one of their blacks were to be seen.

The growing dusk obliterated objects from view at a short distance, and shut off the face of the lagoon. They concluded the obvious at once —that, once their backs had been turned, the blacks had deserted. And a moment later they saw they had guessed only too well.

From the shelter of the coconut grove to the left five shadowy figures broke cover, and dashed off through the dusk in the direction of the bush. About twenty yards behind them ran a sixth figure —the head boy, Abonga.

With an exclamation of anger, Tinker drew his revolver, as though to send a shot after them, but Blake quickly raised his hand.

"Not that, my lad. It will do no good, and may only do harm. Let them go. In a way, I am not sorry, for it means that whatever is going to develop will do so more quickly.

"It will be turn about for us to-night, Tinker, and a keen look-out in addition. Not knowing what has occurred here, we can't guess what will happen, but we can prepare for it. At any rate, we must eat, so let's prepare something."

Together they built a small fire, and got out their few remaining supplies. First they made a thin broth for the captain, and after that boiled some rice for themselves.

When the last morsel had disappeared, and their few utensils washed up, Blake filled his pipe, and they sat down close to the little shack where the raving captain lay.

Darkness had long since descended upon them, and the great brilliant tropical stars blazed overhead as they had blazed all through the ages.

The glorious Southern Cross shone in all its splendour almost directly above them, and in the lagoon the whole studded bowl was reflected in golden perfection.

From the jungle behind them came all the medley of sweet and spicy smells which sweep across the islands at night, borne along by the soft night breeze which sobbed gently through the rustling palms near at hand.

From time to time brilliant streaks of phosphorescence shot across the face of the lagoon like silver-tipped arrows, as some tiny fish rose from the deep and went on its adventurous way.

From the far distance came the sound of the lazily rolling surf against the atoll, and from still farther in the depths of the bush the mournful cry of a night bird.

It was an exquisite night, enwrapping an exquisite spot set in a tropical sea of purple and studded gold, and only the drifting smoke from the smouldering ruins behind them told the two watchers that it was also the home of tragedy and blood lust.

They talked together in low tones until the captain's mutterings subsided, and he fell into a fitful sleep. Then Blake jerked his head in the direction of the shack.

"Better turn in first, my lad. I will keep watch until midnight, and then call you."

"All right, guv'nor," answered the lad obediently, as he rose; "but if you feel fagged, I don't mind taking first watch."

"No, my lad. I will take it. You have had a hard day, so get all the rest you can. Good-night!"

The lad echoed his master's words and disappeared through the low opening which marked the way into the lean-to they had erected. Then Blake refilled his pipe, and prepared himself for his solitary vigil.

It was just nine o'clock when Tinker had turned in, and for a full hour after that Blake sat motionless, puffing at his pipe and pondering on all that had happened.

Though wrapped in his thoughts, he was subconsciously listening constantly for any strange sound which might mark the passage of something alien to the pulsating jungle life about him.

He had been sitting alone for perhaps an hour before a low, rustling noise in the direction of the coconut grove jerked him from his reverie and set every sense on edge.

The noise grew more distinct each moment, and, while realising that it might only be some prowling jungle creature, Blake grew more alert than ever, and held his revolver ready.

Some subtle prescience held him rigid when, a few minutes later, it stopped as mysteriously as it had begun. Yet he knew that whatever it was, it lay but a few yards from him. Behind which shrub or tree it might be he could not tell.

Perhaps that rustling bush straight ahead was moved by a human hand, and not by the night breeze. Perhaps a pair of dark eyes were peering forth at him from the leafy security.

Where he sat beside the dying embers of the fire Blake was dimly silhouetted. Not a muscle did he move, not an eyelash flickered. He was waiting, waiting, with his long fingers curled caressingly about the butt of his revolver.

None knew better than he the danger he ran. The Solomons had been, and still are, the scene of countless brutal murders, born solely of blood-lust, and no more attractive victim could be found than the lone white man. A steady aim, a single shot from the cover of the trees, a quick retreat into the bush, and it would be all over.

What law could prevail? What revenge taken in that pestilential hole of black and naked crime? To discover the one who did it would be like probing a field of stacked wheat for a rotten kernel, a stack in which all the kernels were rotten.

To punish, all would have to be punished, and what would avail amongst such primitive minds in which right and wrong were blended in a heedless whole?

It took courage to plunge into the jungle with the frail expedition he had headed. It took courage to squat patiently in that grass-plaited hut in the hill village whilst the maddened tribe danced their feast dance, and hurled spears and burning brands.

It took a fine bravery to seize the psychological moment to rush them as Blake and his companions had done; but it took a super-courage to sit before that hastily-erected lean-to, silent, watchful, and waiting, while sudden death might lurk close at hand.

It was the supreme test of iron nerve. It was a moment when the superficially strong would have wilted. Yet at the moment of the greatest tension, when each bush, each leaf seemed to hold its sinister menace, Sexton Blake never moved. What a master of strategy the man was! What a master of himself!

Ten minutes, that seemed like an hour, passed without the noise repeating itself; then, when the suspense was becoming well-nigh unbearable, a terrific crashing broke out so close that for a fleeting second Blake thought he was being rushed by a frenzied horde.

Springing to his feet, with revolver ready for instant use, he called out to Tinker.

The words had barely passed his lips when a sharp report rang out at the edge of the grove, followed by a flash, and the heavy impact of a bullet against the lean-to as it whistled past his ears.

Hard on this Tinker appeared, and stood beside his master ready for what might come. But, though the crashing went on unabated, the cause of it did not break forth from cover, nor were any further shots fired.

It was puzzling to explain. It seemed as though a terrific struggle were taking place close to them; but, whereas the shot showed hostility to Blake, the crashing seemed caused by different hostilities. What could it mean?

As he stood, puzzled, a gasping human cry reached Blake's ears, and, unable longer to stand by while that invisible struggle proceeded, he dashed forward with Tinker at his heels. Straight towards the spot whence the noise came he went, and, on reaching the bushes, thrust them aside with his outstretched revolver.

The crashing was going on immediately before him, but so dark was it at first that he could not see the cause. Half a dozen shadowy forms were struggling in a wild and terrific tangle, but to understand who or why was impossible.

Not until a choking cry for his aid reached him did Blake understand even a little what it all meant. But that cry was from Abonga, his head carrier, and the gasped-out words were:

"Master, I die!"

With one jerk Blake had out his pocket-torch, without which he never travelled, and the light which he flashed on the twisting mass before him lit up a vicious scene.

Seven naked blacks were fighting in a hopeless tangle, seven maddened cannibals, whose rage was being wrecked upon each other. In the melee knives flashed out on every side, axes gleamed dully in more than one direction, and a cheap nickled revolver which was being wielded as a club proved that some of the loot from the store still survived.

And there in the midst of the tangle was the face of Abonga, twisted and distorted from blows and cuts. Three other blacks were beating him unmercifully, while two more were slashing at one which Blake recognised as another of his carriers.

He had no idea what had started it, but Abonga's cry to him for aid seemed proof that at least he had not fired the shot which had come so near to cutting short Blake's existence.

Hard on this came the wondering thought that Abonga may have been the cause of no second shot having been fired, and with the suggestion of his mind Blake acted.

"Come on, my lad," he rapped. "It is up to us to help our men. We may be wrong, but we know them, and it is five to two against them."

He dashed forward with clubbed revolver as he spoke, and in a moment he and Tinker were mixed up in the melee. To fight by any code of reason was out of the question. Now that the torch was extinguished it was impossible to distinguish the features of one combatant from those of another.

It was a case of feel for your man, and when you found him hit out as hard as you could. This plan both Blake and Tinker followed, and when, after a wild five minutes of tearing, hitting, kicking, smashing, and choking turmoil, the combatants separated somewhat, they knew their weight had counted.

Still the fight went on. Blake was now locked in a terrific embrace with a giant black, whose arms seemed endowed with the strength of those of a gorilla.

Tinker was smashing out with the butt of his revolver, and a soft thud told that more than once he had reached his mark.

What Abonga and the other carrier were doing they could not see; but from the sound all about them it was as though a dozen wild beasts were tearing at one another's throats.

Then suddenly in some way the whole party became once more entangled, and, as they thrashed about, seeking and striking in the shadow of that lonely jungle, Blake realised that it was a fight for life.

Something cold and rigid seemed to instil itself into his brain, and lend to his arm double strength. With a supreme heave he wrenched himself free from the terrific grip which held him, then he struck out fiercely, blindly.

That his blow got home he knew, and that it had sent his antagonist hurtling into black unconsciousness he also knew. Not a move did the other make. He lay limp and lifeless.

Panting heavily, Blake leaped clear, and searched for a fresh antagonist. He found him at once, and again became mixed up in a smashing duel of blows.

But Abonga had now overcome his man, and, seeing the fate of their fellows, the rest of the enemy turned and fled into the bush.

The two whites and the two carriers stood panting for a few minutes. None essayed to speak. For the time being white as well as black was the primitive man, victorious in brutal combat over his enemy, and, product of cultured civilisation though he was, Blake's nerves still tingled at the memory of limb to limb, arm to arm, and muscle to muscle.

When his pounding heart had grown quieter, Blake turned to Abonga, whose face he could just make out.

"What is this, Abonga? Why do you fight here? And who fired that shot?"

The black stepped forward and submissively bowed his head. Then he pointed to the prostrate savage whom Blake had conquered.

"Him try murder you. I try him stop. Fight, kill. You come, save!"

"So he was the one who tried to pick me off," mused Blake. Then aloud, "Good boy, Abonga! You come longa hut. Tell me."

He turned as he spoke, broke back through the bushes, and headed for the lean-to, followed by Tinker and the two blacks.

On arriving there he lit his pipe, and, after seating himself, motioned to Abonga to stand before him.

"Now, Abonga, make tell," he ordered.

It was a long story which the black had to tell, and as it was couched in the pidgin English of the islands it would have been utterly unintelligible to the average listener. But, briefly stated in ordinary language, it was as follows:

When Blake and Tinker had gone into the hut to look after the captain, some of the village blacks, who had been observing them from the bush, signalled to the carriers. Before Abonga could prevent them his five companions had started for the bush on the run, dodging along through the coconut grove as they went.

He, Abonga, took after them, not to join them, but to bring them back. That was why Blake and Tinker had seen five figures break cover together, followed by the sixth at some distance behind, and that which he had seen told Blake Abonga was speaking the truth.

The black did not overtake his fellows until they reached the other savages, and, on seeing a council of war was in progress, Abonga stayed. There he heard the full tale of the shooting of Johnson, the trader, of the looting of the station, and of the disastrous attack on the fleeing schooner.

At the same time he listened to a discussion as to what should be done to the little party of whites which had just arrived. Those who were still in the grip of the lust wished to make an immediate attack and then take to the bush.

Others, sobered and therefore saner, counselled moderation. They had intelligence enough to realise that payment for Johnson's death would certainly be exacted, and though they had no moral reasons for moving cautiously, they had no wish to tighten the rope about their own necks.

Abonga's arrival and his arguments in favour of leaving the white party in peace seemed about to bring the decision in this direction, but in the very midst of the discussion several of the maddened savages had seized their weapons and raced on intent upon killing.

With only one carrier to stand by him, Abonga had followed. The shot at Blake had been fired from a needle gun, and it was just as Abonga arrived that the trigger had been pulled. Then followed the fight.

When the black had finished his tale, Blake puffed for some minutes in silence, then he looked up.

"Abonga, you good boy. You speak now."

The black bowed his head and waited.

"Who kill the white man, Abonga?"

"The white magician you seek, master."

"You tell longa truth."

"All truth."

"Who take schooner?"

Abonga raised his arm and spoke.

"Two, three, four days, big boat, plenty people lost in storm here. All go down —plenty, plenty. One man swim longa shore. Stay here. White magician come longa bush. Shoot trader. With other white man run. Take schooner. Sail way longa lagoon. Black fella go mad. Drink, fire. Run longa schooner. White magician send fire-boat. All killed. Plenty, plenty."

As Abonga's voice died, away in an odd whisper, Blake glanced wonderingly at Tinker.

"Did you get all that, my lad?"

"Most of it, guv'nor."

"I wonder if it is true? If he is to be believed, Black McCabe reached here and shot Johnson, as he had threatened to do. During the storm, which we had on our first night a ship seems to have been wrecked on the island, and only one man got ashore.

"He and McCabe seem to have joined forces, and seized the schooner. Then the blacks ran amok, as we already know, and, after looting the station, set off after the schooner.

"Either McCabe or the other white man apparently sent some sort of fireboat into the fleet of canoes, and succeeded in killing most of them. Then they sailed away.

"Our chase after Black McCabe has led us into a disastrous position, my lad. Johnson has been killed, half the village exterminated, the station destroyed, the schooner, our only means of leaving the island, stolen, and, to cap all, we are left while McCabe sails we don't know where. Rather an attractive state of affairs to say the least."

"It is, if Abonga tells the truth," answered Tinker grimly.

"He is speaking as he knows, I am certain," responded Blake. "Our present position here is very precarious, but since we can count on his loyalty for the present, at least, we may pull through safely until the blacks become sane again.

"But though every trick so far seems to have been taken by McCabe, I swear that I shall not rest until I have come to grips with him, and landed him where he belongs. I swear it by poor Johnson, who fell a victim to his murderous hand. He is a thief, a murderer, a renegade. I will stay on his trail until I get him."

Blake now lay at full length on the ground, and for some minutes kept the glasses unwaveringly on the steamer.

THE EIGHTH CHAPTER. *The Arrival of Yvonne.*

THREE days passed —three long, galling, chafing days, yet busy ones withal. There was much done which had no bearing on his own affairs; but, being the only white man to assume authority and bring back a sense of order and fitness to the trading station, Blake did it.

On the morning following the fight in the coconut-grove, he sent Abonga, to the blacks in the bush commanding them to return and set to work on the ruins. After some delay, they appeared one by one, silent and wondering at the strange white man who moved so quietly yet so confidently.

The first thing to be done was to find the trader's body and to bury him. Then Blake set the whole force clearing up the debris and erecting shacks.

In the work to which he drove them, they forgot that which had gone before, and once completely under his domination, worked more or less honestly.

And so the three days passed until the fourth —a day which was to be crowded with surprising events. To begin with, Captain Weeks came out of the fever which had been consuming him, and, though still extremely weak, began to mend.

The morning was still young and the blacks were already busy at work on the new shacks, when Abonga came running to Blake with news written upon his dusky countenance. He pointed excitedly towards the lagoon, and following the direction of his outstretched arm, Blake saw a sturdy whaleboat nearing the beach.

In it he could make out five men, one of whom appeared to be a white man. Followed by Tinker and Abonga, he hurried towards the strip of silver sand, and as the boat got still nearer, he saw that his eyes had not deceived him.

The man in the stern was the white sailor who had taken the news of the disaster to the Kara Maru to the island sixty miles away. He waved his hand as he recognised Blake, and called out:

"Glad to see you back safe, Mr. Blake. How is the captain?"

"He has had a bad attack of fever, Ford, but is mending rapidly. But I am glad to see you back, I can tell you. Many things have happened since you have been away."

The seaman looked at Blake sharply as the boat's nose ran up on the beach; then he sprang out.

"Anything serious, sir? Any thing to do with the schooner? Where is she?"

"Come along to the camp, Ford, and I will tell you all."

Leaving Abonga to see after the boat, Blake led the way back through the coconut grove. As they emerged from it, and came within view of the station, the seaman gave a gasp of surprise, but said nothing. It was evident to him that something indeed had happened; but a long experience among the islands made it not difficult for him to guess to a certain extent what that something was.

Blake kept on until he reached the lean-to where the captain lay, and when the greetings were over between the two seamen, he went straight to the point.

"Now, Ford," he said, filling his pipe, "as I told you, much has happened here. From the blacks we heard that a boat had gone ashore on the reef outside, and with the exception of one man, all had been lost. We also heard vaguely that a seaman had left the schooner and had taken the news of the disaster to the nearest island, where there is a wireless.

"Tell us all you know first, then I will relate what has happened. As Captain Weeks has been delirious until this morning, he knows nothing as yet so be explicit."

The sailor began with the coming of the hurricane, and related all that had happened up to the time when, with four blacks as a crew, he had set off for the island sixty miles away to take the news. He told the name of the lost steamer, and related how the one survivor had been saved. Then he went on:

"We had a smooth trip to the other island, sir; but on landing, stove in the bow of the whaleboat. As soon as I delivered the news to the magistrate there, I set to work to mend the boat, and that was why I was gone a week instead of two or three days. We had a fair run back, but when I got inside the lagoon, and saw that the schooner was gone, I thought you had left without me."

"The schooner gone!" cried the captain, trying to sit up in his excitement. "What do you mean, Ford? Where is Johnson, and, what has happened?"

"Steady, captain!" said Blake quietly. "As I said, a great deal has happened while you have been ill. You must prepare yourself for something of a shock, and when I have told you all, we can discuss our plans. Let me see, you can't remember much after our escape from the hut in the bush, do you?"

"Not a thing,"

"Then, listen! Johnson is dead. He was killed by the man we were after, Black McCabe. At least, that is the story the blacks tell, and I am inclined to believe it.

"Hard on that the blacks rose, but not before Black McCabe and the man who was saved from the wrecked steamer had joined forces. They escaped, and in some way got control of the schooner. They must have overpowered the solitary seaman, and overawed the Kanaka crew. Anyway, they accomplished it someway.

"After that the blacks here attacked it, but, as near as I can make out, they were repulsed by McCabe and his companion, and by the use of a fireboat, half of them were killed.

"Then the schooner was worked through the lagoon passage, and has sailed away to heaven only knows where. Here a frightful orgy of burning and looting took place, and when we got back from the bush, the place was in ruins.

"I must confess that with McCabe gone, the schooner stolen, and us practically marooned here, the prospect looks bad, but we have not lost out yet. At any rate, captain, you must not worry about your ship. If she is gone for good, you shall be reimbursed fully."

For some time the captain lay silent after Blake had finished his tale. It was easy to see that the news had been a hard blow to him, and, weakened as he was by the fever, he took it more to heart than he would have done had he been strong and hearty. His lip was trembling, and his eyes were wet as he looked up, but his smile was brave.

"It —it hits me a little to think of the old Island Queen in the hands of a couple of tarnal pirates," he said. "But what is done is done. As you say, Mr. Blake, they seem to hold four aces, but let me get my hands on them, and, by heavens, I'll show them what it costs to play the piracy game on board my ship."

"And we will get our hands on them, captain. This but adds to the reckoning between Black McCabe and myself, and I promise you he will yet be amply punished. I shall not rest until I have run him to earth.

"But we must consider our next move, and how we are to get away from the island. That is essential if we are to catch our man, for every day that we are marooned here, means a day in McCabe's favour."

"You are right, Mr. Blake. If I had not been knocked out by the fever, we might have been away by now."

"You must not blame yourself, captain. We —"

Blake broke off, and glanced round as a shadow filled the low entrance. It was Abonga, and for the second time that morning Blake saw that he was the bearer of news.

"What is it?" he asked quickly.

"Schooner outside, master. Beat longa way, longa way. No come in."

For a moment Blake stared at him in astonishment, then turned back to the others.

"Abonga says there is a schooner outside beating about, but that she shows no signs of coming into the lagoon. Stay here with the captain, Ford. Tinker, bring the glasses. We will go over on the hill to the right of the lagoon, and have a look at her. We may be able to get away in her."

While Tinker rummaged for the glasses, Blake followed Abonga outside, but from where he was standing, could see nothing of the schooner of which the black had spoken. He stood gazing impatiently until Tinker appeared; then, with the black leading the way, all three set off at a run for the hill to the right which overlooked the palm-locked lagoon, and gave a command of the sea beyond.

As they reached the summit, and came out upon a small clearing, Blake turned seawards, and swept the blue water with eager eyes. Sure enough, as the black had said, there was a ship beating about off the reef, but she was no schooner. She was a Chinese junk. There could be no mistaking that awkward shape, with the great, high poop and the square, matting sails.

Blake reached for the glasses without a word, and trained them on her. Even as he did so, the junk came about, and dropped anchor Then followed a strange series of movements by those on board, which were only too plain to Blake, but which had to be guessed at by Tinker, filled in by the phrases Blake flung at him from time to time.

"Anchor down, my lad. Now she comes round. All hands furling the sails. Ah! By thunder, Tinker, her stern has come round, and if she isn't the same junk we saw at Port Moresby when we were there, I am a Dutchman. She is, she is, my lad, the Fen-ho —I can read her name.

"Now, what on earth are they doing? A big winch is being got into position. What the — Ah, there come a half dozen Chinks along the deck carrying something. It is —yes, by thunder, it is a diving-suit, Tinker!"

For a brief moment he lowered the glasses, relinquishing them to Tinker as he turned to Abonga.

"Did black fella tell where ship go down, Abonga?" he asked quickly.

"Yes, master. Longa way ship."

"Just there?" And Blake pointed with his hand.

The black nodded. Blake's hand was reaching out for the glasses again when Tinker lowered them and swung sharply, with excitement dancing in his eyes.

"Quick, guv'nor!" he cried. "Take them and have a look at that fat Chinaman who is directing the men at the winch. If we haven't met him before I'll eat my hat."

Blake took the glasses and trained them once more on the junk. Slowly he brought them into line until he had them focussed on the crowd upon the winch. For a moment they wavered about until he found the stout Celestial to whom Tinker had referred, then he gave a start of amazement.

"Scott! Tinker, is it possible?"

"You think so too, then, guv'nor?"

"I think that fat Chinaman is none other than the shrewd, cunning Celestial, San, who was Prince Wu Ling's right hand man, Tinker."

"And that is whom I thought, guv'nor," exclaimed the lad, dancing with excitement. "What on earth do you suppose he is doing there?"

"I can't make out yet, Tinker; but if San is behind it, it must be something worth while. By thunder, I believe I have it. They are fixing the diving-dress. One of them intends going down.

"I really believe they have been beating back and forth until they have found where the Kara Maru lies, and they are going down to her. Now, I wonder what they are after? Something they have no right to, I'll warrant.

"Tinker, hurry back to the shack and tell Ford, the seaman, to get the whaleboat ready. If things go on as they are, I think I shall go out and interview our old friend San.

"Scott! I'd like to know what went down on the Kara Maru which was important enough to bring that wily Celestial over here on a private diving expedition. He must have made his arrangements as soon as the news was known, and the speed at which they are working proves they are anxious to get what they are after and sail away before anybody else turns up.

"That means they expect another ship on the scene —probably one will be sent by the owners of the Kara Maru to investigate matters. Then we will stand a chance of getting away soon."

Already Tinker was making for the shack on a run and, squatting on the ground, Blake kept the glasses trained on the junk. He saw one of the Chinese seamen advance and get into the diving-suit. Then he saw the stout one, whom he could swear was San, step forward and talk earnestly for some minutes to the man in the suit.

While a couple of men hung a long ladder over the side, the helmet was screwed on the diving-suit, and a moment later the diver was going down the ladder into the blue, shark-infested depths where lay the Kara Maru.

Ten minutes —fifteen minutes passed before the diver reappeared, and as he climbed back up the ladder, Blake saw two men spring forward to unscrew the helmet. Then San held a long conversation with him.

For a quarter of an hour they talked on and gesticulated. Tinker returned to report that the whaleboat was being got ready, but Blake motioned him to silence. Not for a single moment did he relax his gaze from the junk, and when the helmet was screwed on over the diver's head for the second time he watched keenly.

Again the diver went over the side, and again he disappeared below the surface. Another twenty minutes passed before he reappeared and was hauled back on deck. When his helmet had once more been removed, Blake saw San lean forward and ask a question.

He saw the diver shake his head and talk rapidly for some moments. As he finished, San leaped into the air and came down again gesticulating like a madman. For five solid minutes he talked violently to the diver, and more than once Blake thought he was about to push the man over the side.

Then something happened which not only caused intense excitement on board the junk, but raised a wave of hope in Blake's breast. Far away on the horizon a cloud of black smoke appeared, and, as he watched it, Blake saw that it was steadily becoming more distinct.

A steamer of some kind was coming up hand over hand, and appeared to be heading straight for the island of Rubilinga. That the Chinese thought so, too, was evident from their actions.

Blake saw San hurry away and return a few moments later carrying a telescope. This he trained on the smoke and, after studying it for some time, handed the glass to one of his companions and hurried back to the winch.

He made a curt motion to the man who still sat in the diving dress. The latter got out of it with alacrity, and to Blake's surprise San himself got into it. The helmet was at once screwed on, and making a gesture to those at the pump, he went over the side.

Blake divided his attention between the junk and the smoke on the horizon. As the minutes passed he began to make out a funnel beneath the smoke, then the hull of the ship herself came into view, and he was able to distinguish that she was a small steamer of some sort.

Then he turned the glasses back to the junk, and kept them on her until he saw San appear above the water and grasp the rungs of the ladder which hung over the side. Clumsily the diver made his way over the side and sat down while two men unscrewed the helmet.

Then he got out of the suit and, standing up, issued a curt order. In a moment all was hustle. Blake saw half a dozen men spring towards the sails, while others manned the winch and began winding up the anchor.

Speedily they worked, and when the anchor came up, dripping, from the bottom, the sails filled out, sending the clumsy craft heeling slightly. She was at once brought round, and just as Tinker could make out the hull of the steamer with naked eye, the junk gathered way and headed in another direction.

Blake now lay at full length on the ground, and for some minutes kept the glasses unwaveringly on the steamer. Watching him closely, Tinker could see that something was causing his master great excitement.

The tense rise and fall of the powerful shoulders, the dilation of the finely-cut nostril, the knuckles white with the force of his grip, all told their own tale. Whatever it was, it lay in the rapidly approaching steamer; and just as Tinker himself was beginning to get a startling suggestion as to the reason, Blake dropped the glasses and turned his head upwards.

"My lad," he cried in ringing tones, "it is unbelievable. Yet it is so —it is so. That steamer is the Fleur-de-Lys, Mademoiselle Yvonne's yacht.

"To the whaleboat at top speed. I must know if she is aboard."

· · ·

What an extraordinary situation it had all developed into! So thought Blake, as the whaleboat shot across the limpid waters of the lagoon, heading for the passage to the sea beyond.

It had been strange enough to find himself on the savage and almost unknown island of Rubilinga, in pursuit of a London criminal. But since that morning but a week past, how events had moved.

The expedition into the wild jungle —the fight with the wilder cannibals of the hills —the piracy of the schooner —the shooting of the trader —the looting of the station —the escape of Black McCabe, and, with him, a man whom as yet Blake little dreamed was in that part of the world —Dr. Huxton Rymer.

And now had come a mysterious Chinese junk, in charge of one of the most cunning Celestials who had ever come out of the secret East —San, the former lieutenant of the late Prince Wu Ling, head of that colossal organisation known as the Brotherhood of the Yellow Beetle, and one of the greatest foes with whom Sexton Blake had ever crossed swords.

Not only that, but San had lost no time in sending down a diver to the wrecked Kara Maru, and had even made one descent himself. To add to the mystery of it all, a steamer had appeared on the scene —a steamer which had sent the junk sailing away, and which Blake now knew beyond doubt was that slim, graceful yacht, the Fleur-de-Lys, property of Mademoiselle Yvonne.

What did it all mean? Was Rubilinga, a solitary savage island in the Solomons, but a coincidental meeting-place for different threads of intrigue? Had the fates in their mysterious way chosen it as the one spot to witness the course of several separate and distinct dramas?

Was there more than pure chance in the almost simultaneous arrival at that savage island of Yvonne and San the Celestial? Had it any bearing on the loss of the Kara Maru? Was it connected in any way with Blake's own mission to the island? If so, where was the link connecting them? Could it be anything about Johnson the trader?

Little did Blake dream that the link connecting the seemingly separate purposes was that sole survivor of the Kara Maru, the man who had apparently joined forces with Black McCabe in the capture of the schooner. He had accepted the meagre reports of the survivor at their face value, and not until some time later was he to discover the identity of that individual.

From those things his mind went off to Yvonne herself —that slim, misty-eyed girl who had twined herself about his heart in such a tenderly unyielding hold.

The intense blue of the sea seemed harsh to the soft blue of her eyes, and the ruddiest gold of the living coral was dross to the shimmering bronze of her hair. No slim young palm stood as gracefully straight as did she —no blazing orchid of the jungle was more crimson than her lips.

She was to Blake different to all other women —a girl who, despite all his rigidly-repressed nature, had struck deep into the austere thoughts of his mind. With nearly all others he was a cold machine of mathematical precision —with her he was endowed with singing life, which throbbed achingly when he gazed into the wistful eyes which were hers.

Not since they had met so strangely during Blake's investigation of the famous Death Club had they met, and, as the whaleboat shot through the passage into the open sea, revealing the slim, familiar lines of the Fleur-de-Lys, a flood of feeling overwhelmed Blake as his eyes eagerly sought the rail.

And then suddenly a dainty figure in white could be descried leaning negligently over the side with a pair of glasses trained on the oncoming whaleboat. There could be no mistake about that graceful poise —there could be no mistake about the dull gold beneath the widespread sun-helmet. It was Yvonne.

Blake relaxed with very relief; and not until he did so did he realise how strained had been his every sense. Yet he was filled with a strange wild joy, and he was not ashamed of it.

On went the boat, dashing into the rolling blue and sending the white-edged waves to either side in little bursts of spray, which caught the sun in a thousand ways, to fall like myriads of diamonds into a bed of sapphire. It was but a phase of that intense beauty which enwraps the South Pacific.

At last the yacht came within hail, and Blake, who had been watching for the moment when Yvonne should lower her glasses, smiled when she did so. He could now see the wonder, the disbelief in her attitude. He could see her hand drawn across her eyes, as though she were trying to convince herself that it was but a dream, that picture she had seen through her glasses.

He saw her give one glance of her blue eyes in the direction of the whaleboat, then her hand went up, and though he could not hear her, he could imagine her silvery voice ringing out in clear command.

Nor was he mistaken. Almost immediately he saw Captain Vaughan appear on the bridge and the white foam at the stern give way to a wake of marbled green and purple as her screw stopped. Then he saw Hendricks, the sturdy mate, directing half a dozen white-clad sailors in the lowering of the gangway.

His own boat shot forward at the same instant, he sprang over the gunwale, landing lightly on the platform of the gangway. Then without haste he ascended, though his pulses urged him to cover the distance in mighty leaps.

Up, up he went, resolutely keeping his eyes on the gangway; then he arrived at the top and, turning slowly, found himself face to face with —Yvonne.

A moment later her soft hands were in his —his shoulders were heaving with the same emotion which swept over him —her eyes caught his and held them, drawing him deep down into their misty azure depths.

And so they stood, both too full of that exquisite throbbing emotion to speak.

Blake found himself face to face with Yvonne, and
their hands met in a tight clasp.

A dainty figure in white could be descried leaning
negligently against the wall. It was Yvonne.

IT was the arrival of Tinker and Pedro hard on their master's heels which broke the tension between Blake and Yvonne. When the lad's cheery face appeared over the side she gave an embarrassed little laugh, and slowly withdrew her hands from Blake's grasp.

She greeted Tinker warmly, but it was in the heavy folds of Pedro's great neck that her flushed face was buried until the crimson flame which had suffused her had fled. Only then did she straighten up and become once more the cool, gracious hostess.

"I am so dumbfounded at meeting you here I can hardly believe it," she said, with a shy little laugh at Blake. "I thought you were in London."

"And I am quite as surprised at seeing you here, Yvonne," he smiled. "Fancy meeting at this forsaken island of all places. But what brings you? Is it permitted to ask?"

Yvonne nodded.

"Yes. In fact, I am not sure that I am not glad to see you in more ways than one. I am here for a purpose. It is nothing of my own, but I have placed my yacht at the disposal of a friend. But here he comes now, and after I have introduced you to him and his charming wife we can talk."

Blake followed the direction of her eyes and saw, approaching along the deck, a tall, thin, slightly-stooped man of middle age, and a small, delicately-featured woman who may have been forty-five, but looked thirty. They came on leisurely until within a few paces of the group by the gangway, when Yvonne motioned to them.

"Come here," she said gaily. "I have a wonderful surprise for you, dear friends."

The pair smiled indulgently and did as she bade them.

"Mr. Blake," went on Yvonne. "let me present you to a very dear friend of my mother's, Mrs. Lamport, and to Captain Lamport, of whom beware. If he gets you cornered in the smoking-room he will keep you at the chess-board until you drop."

Blake smilingly bowed in acknowledgment of the introductions.

"I am afraid Yvonne will ruin my reputation," laughed Captain Lamport. "But don't you pay any attention to her, Mr. Blake. She is only jealous because she always loses."

"Indeed, I won a game the night we left Brisbane," she protested.

"Is this the Mr. Blake —Mr. Sexton Blake?" asked Mrs. Lamport, turning her twinkling grey eyes on Yvonne.

She nodded.

"Yes."

"I have heard a great deal about you, Mr. Blake," went on Mrs. Lamport, with a spark of mischief in her eyes. "It was not all from the papers, either. I think it was —"

"No tales out of school, Aunt Alice," put in Yvonne, blushing deliciously. "You will make him vain."

"You don't look a bit like I always imagined you did, Mr. Blake," went on the elder woman. "I thought you would have a fierce expression?"

"And haven't I?" laughed Blake.

"Not a bit. You look like —"

"A lamb," supplemented her husband.

"And warranted to feed from the hand," put in Yvonne maliciously. "But come, friends, let us have tea. I have told them to serve it on deck, and I see Alec approaching to call us."

Laughing and chatting, they made their way to the broad after-deck where, under a wide-spread awning, tea had been served. It was a picture not soon to be forgotten that was spread before them.

Off to port lay the island, rising darkly green from the deep blue ocean. All around the atoll the surf rolled gently, leaving a tiny ribbon of white where the coral repelled it. Overhead spread the limitless azure of a cloudless tropical sky, reflected in the ocean about them.

And the yacht! Slim and graceful she lay rocking gently in the swell —a picture of spotless white and shimmering brass. What with the dainty white dresses of the women, the stiffer white of the men, the low, wide, wicker deck chairs, and the silently moving white-clad stewards, it was a picture of tropical ease and comfort hard to surpass.

Yvonne was charming as a hostess, and what with the banter which was tossed back and forth between her, the captain and Blake it was a merry party. The others were content to listen and sip their iced Russian tea appreciatively.

A little later Captain Vaughan was able to leave the bridge, and when he appeared the greeting between him and Blake was very warm indeed, for, since the old days when they had been pitted against each other in stern combat, they had passed through many dangers together, and had become fast friends.

Not until the tea-things had been cleared away, and the smoke of Yvonne's dainty cigarette had blended with the heavier smoke from the cigars of the three men, did she broach the subject which had been briefly referred to at the gangway.

"And now, sir," she said, looking at Blake with eyes softly veiled, "what have you to say for yourself? Why do we find you in such a spot as this?"

"That is easily answered, Yvonne. I came here after a man —a criminal whom I followed from London. He has led me a long chase, and I haven't got him yet."

"Is he on the island?"

"He was, but he has escaped. Not only that, but he took the very schooner we came in."

She sat up suddenly.

"We saw a ship —a junk, I think —near the island as we came up. Was that it? If so, the yacht is at your disposal. We could overtake it in no time."

Blake shook his head.

"No, that was not it. It has been gone from the island over three days. But the whole story is long and complicated. Supposing you tell me first why you have come to Rubilinga? Then, if you care to hear, I shall tell you what has happened to us."

"How long did you say you had been here?"

"Eight days."

"Then —why, yes, you must have been here when the Kara Maru went down. Were you?" she asked excitedly.

"I was here, but did not witness it. I heard about it when we came back from an expedition into the bush."

"But she really did go down here, didn't she?"

"Oh, there is no doubt about that, In fact, I think I know the spot."

Yvonne turned to Captain Lamport.

"Will you tell him, captain?" she asked.

"With pleasure," he replied, straightening up. "It won't take long, Mr. Blake, and from what Yvonne has said you can guess it has to do with the Kara Maru.

"I should say before I begin that I am the president of the Eastern Pearl Fishing Co., with fishing boats at Thursday Island and headquarters at Brisbane. About two weeks ago our manager at Thursday Island found one of the most unique pearls ever discovered.

"It was not of an extraordinary size, but some freak of formation had caused throughout it a crimson shade which, when held close to the eye, looked like living flame. It was the most remarkable specimen of its kind I ever saw or heard of, and needless to say I set the value very high.

"Owing to that fact, and also on account of suspicions held by our manager at Thursday Island that two Chinamen who had disappeared from there had left with the intent to get possession of the pearl, I decided to send it on at once to Lord Cambrey, our honorary president in England.

"As it was impossible for me to go myself, I chose for the mission our head clerk at Brisbane, a young fellow in whom I had the greatest confidence. He received the pearl from me, and started for England via Hong Kong. He sailed on the Kara Maru.

"A week ago a wireless message came through saying that the Kara Maru had been wrecked in the Solomons, in the hurricane which swept over this part at that time. She must have been blown a long way off her course. The message said there had been one survivor only —a seaman named Carr —and that his story was that the Kara Maru had lost her propeller early in the storm.

"I could hardly believe the message, and went to see the Brisbane agents of the steamer. They were inclined to accept it at its face value, since they had had no news whatever of the Kara Maru from the time she left Brisbane. At any rate, they began at once to get ready a ship to come on here and investigate matters.

"They offered to take me along, and I half-way accepted. But that same day we had a wireless from Yvonne saying she would arrive in the yacht from Sydney that night. When she heard the story she placed the yacht at our disposal, and after getting aboard we came on at once. I expect the company steamer will be here to-morrow or next day."

"Then, in your opinion, the pearl went down with the Kara Maru?" asked Blake.

"Yes. I firmly believe the crimson pearl is in the pouch around Ferguson's neck, and if he is still in the ship we should get it. It is worth about two hundred thousand pounds, so I think the risk worth taking.

"Captain Vaughan has already taken soundings, so if the Kara Maru is not lying in deeper water than we, it ought not to be difficult to reach her. There are seventeen fathoms here."

"She is not in deeper water," said Blake quietly. "Moreover, I am quite certain that a diver will be able to reach her. In fact, I may tell you that your diver will not be the first to go down to her."

"What do you mean?" cried Captain Lamport and Yvonne in one voice.

Blake lifted his arm and pointed over the rail.

"Do you see that smudge on the horizon?" he asked.

They nodded.

"That is the junk which you saw when you came up. She has already had a diver down three times."

"A junk!" exclaimed Captain Lamport excitedly, rising and moving to the rail. "That means she is manned by Chinese, and Chinese were after the crimson pearl. By heavens, they have anticipated us! They have secured the pearl. Yvonne, we must overtake them at once!"

"Wait a moment, captain," put in Blake quietly. "I said they had had a diver down, but I did not say they had succeeded in their purpose. On the contrary, I am inclined to think that they did not succeed. At the same time, I should not be at all surprised if the pearl was the bait which drew them here, reason for thinking that is this:

"Through the glasses I had a good look at the Chinaman who was the leader. Tinker also saw him, and both of us were certain we recognised him. He is one of the deepest Celestials in the East. You will know whom I mean when I tell you that it is the Chinaman, San, formerly the right-hand man of Prince Wu Ling, the Chinese fanatic."

"Then if that is so, I'll wager he came here for nothing but your pearl, captain," said Yvonne. "But what makes you think he did not get it, Mr. Blake?"

"His actions. They were not those of a man who had succeeded in his purpose. I am certain he intended going down again, but you drove him away. As soon as you were sighted San himself made a hurried descent, and as soon as he came up the junk got away.

"Of course, I am not at all certain that he failed, but I think he did. At any rate, if he did he is gone for good, but if he didn't he will return. He will hardly suspect your purpose. He will think your arrival but a chance, and will beat about until you go. But there is one way to settle the matter."

"You mean?"

"To make a descent at once. By the way, have you a regular diver with you?"

"No," answered Captain Lamport. "I had a little experience of it some years ago, and as it is a matter I wish to keep as quiet as possible, I thought I would go down myself."

"If you care to have me do so, I should be glad to go," said Blake.

"Indeed, I should very much. There is a risk, you know."

"You mean sharks?"

"Yes."

"I know. I am quite prepared to chance any there may be about. But if I am to go down I think it wise to lose no time. I know the exact spot where the Chinese went down, and as I am certain they had the correct location, I think we can do no better than to try there too. If you will give orders to go ahead slowly, Captain Vaughan, I will go up on the bridge with you, and show you where it is."

Captain Vaughan rose at once, and not only Blake but the whole party followed him up to the bridge. He signalled the engine-room for half-speed ahead and, with Blake standing just behind the man at the wheel directing him, the Fleur-de-Lys glided slowly ahead towards the spot where Blake had seen the junk anchored.

On reaching it Blake held up his hand, Captain Vaughan rang a signal, and raising his voice, shouted to Hendricks to drop the anchor. A moment later they were swinging gently against the cable, while all hands leaned over the side and gazed with fascination at the blue waters, which held in their embrace the answer to the riddle which had brought them there.

As the afternoon was already well advanced, and Blake wished to make at least one descent that day, no time was lost in getting the diving gear on deck. The party descended from the bridge to the maindeck, while the sailors were busy rigging up the pump and arranging the suit.

When all was ready, Blake got into it, and sat down for the helmet to be screwed on. Not until the last moment was the heavy middle eye-piece screwed into place, then, rising, he grasped the top rungs of the ladder which had been hung over the side.

For a moment he stood so, gazing through the heavy plate-glass in the front of the helmet at the little group who stood watching his descent. One brief second his gaze rested on Yvonne, whose blue eyes were weighted with anxiety, for Captain Lamport's remarks about sharks were still ringing in her ears.

Then, touching the axe and lamp which hung at his waist, Blake signed to the men at the rope, and started down the ladder. Down, down, he went, until his lead-weighted boots touched the water. Still further he descended until the water had reached his waist, his shoulders, his neck. Another step and he found himself beneath the surface in the arms of the ocean —in a world of dim light and teeming strange life.

He could dimly make out the hull of the yacht as he descended. It curved away from him gradually until the shadow ended at the keel, then he reached the end of the ladder.

For a moment he hung there gazing to right, to left, above and below him. For a moment he wondered just what those coral-lined depths held. For a moment he allowed the wonder of it all to engulf him; then, releasing his grip on the ladder, he started downwards at the mercy of a thin line, a thin tube of rubber and the creatures of the boundless ocean.

Down, down, went Blake into a region of ever growing darkness. The twilight near the surface became but a darkling grey, and still he had not reached the bottom. As yet he was suffering no discomfort. The pressure seemed but ordinary, and the air-pump was working splendidly.

More than once shoals of small fishes flashed past him, their globular eyes peering for a moment at the strange creature which had invaded their home. Hard after them would rush the long grey shape of a predatory fish, and in turn would flee from the strange "fish" with eyes greater than any it had seen before.

Though their sudden appearances startled him for a moment, Blake did not mind them, knowing they were harmless. The only danger from them was that the hunting fish might pierce the air-tube and create trouble.

But what he watched for was the great king of the deep, which held undisputed sway over all the others —the long, powerful shark.

Should he run up against one who was of the fighting breed, and who chose to dispute his right to be there, well —it promised one of the most unpleasant moments one could well imagine.

But at last he landed on the coral bed beneath him, and so far had no signs of any. For the time being all thought of danger went from his mind, and he stood braced against a cliff of crimson coral, gazing about him.

It was for all the world as though he stood on a mountain slops beneath the ocean. And, in fact, that is exactly what it was. Before him stretched the coral bed, dipping downwards until it was lost in the depths; above him the living coral rose, irregularly, until it also was lost to view, but which he knew went to form the atoll at the surface.

To right and left it broke away roughly, forming miniature valleys and cliffs. And there to the right, resting in a short coral valley was a huge black shape, which made his heart leap. Like a miner stumbling along a rocky canyon, Blake made his way towards it.

From time to time, as he dropped into some crevice between the points, it was lost to view; but ever as he rose again it appeared. And at last, when he climbed the last rise before the valley in which it lay, he knew that he had found that which he sought.

The great shape was a sunken steamer, which had found her grave in that coral valley, and on the bow he could make out the name Kara Maru. So far the tale he had heard had been true. With much difficulty he moved along beside her until he reached the overhanging stern.

He had a definite object in view, and wished to put it to the test before going aboard. No sooner had he rounded the stern and gazed upwards, than he was able to do so. For the second time he found proof of the story told by the solitary survivor, for the propeller of the Kara Maru was missing.

After examining it thoroughly, Blake made his way back as he had just come, until the rising coral brought him close to the bows where a great jagged hole could be seen —the hole which had been the death wound of the ship.

Using both the coral wall of the valley and the side of the steamer to assist him, he slowly worked his way upwards, until at last he was able to pull himself over the side. He found himself standing on the saloon deck, just opposite the saloon entrance, and for the first time noticed how evenly the steamer lay. There was scarcely any slope to the deck.

For a few moments he stood there, going over in his mind the last words he had had with Captain Lamport just before he had descended. The captain had shown him a plan of the ship in which was marked in blue pencil the location of the cabin in which Ferguson had travelled.

Both the captain and Blake had agreed that were Ferguson's body not in the cabin, the chances of locating him would be very slim indeed; but there was a chance that he may have been caught in his bunk when the ship struck, and on that chance had Captain Lamport builded.

Standing where he was Blake knew, from his study of the map, that Cabin 20 was just beneath him, and that if San's descent had been successful, he too had stood where Blake now stood. Then, with a last look about him he went forward, and worked his way through the saloon entrance.

He found the descent easy —easy when compared with the sharp, dangerous coral over which he had just come. It was necessary for him to stop from time to time to draw the signal rope and air-tube after him, particularly when turning into the passage which would take him to the cabin he sought. But the men on the deck of the Fleur-de-Lys were paying out the rope and tube at exactly the right speed, and his difficulty on that score was small.

Down the passage he went, searching by the light of the electric torch he had lighted for the number of the cabin he sought. More than one open door he passed, and through the water which filled it could see sights which sent throbs of sorrow through him. But those cabins held nothing which was a part of his work. It was for the company which was sending a steamer to attend to.

Right down near the end of the passage he finally came to an open door, and raising his torch read the number. It was twenty. Without pausing he pushed through, but had barely taken a couple of steps when the lead weighted soles of his diving dress came in contact with something on the floor.

Bending down he lowered the torch, and there before him saw two things which caused a thrill to run through him. One was a long bladed kris of a very strong description, the other was the body of a Chinaman fully dressed.

Slowly Blake straightened up and moved to one side. Passing the body of the Chinaman, he kept on until he came to the bunks. Once more he raised the torch, and started forward as the light fell on the face of a white man who lay in the bunk.

Instinctively his eyes sought the throat and, peering through the thick glass of the diving helmet, he saw that the garments were open; that not only was there no pouch about the neck, but that a great wound still remained in the breast.

Slowly he backed up until he was in the middle of the cabin. Bending again he picked up the knife and, with a last look at the Chinaman on the floor, was turning to go, when he felt something strike his head. At first he thought it was a fish which had worked its way into the cabin, but as it came round in front of him he could make out the flat form of a lifebelt which had broken loose.

He half raised his arm to push it to one side and go on, when just as he did so he saw something stamped on it which caused him instead to catch it and draw it close.

What he had seen was only a number, but with the sight had come a sudden recollection to Blake, which caused him to stand rigid with the memory aroused.

As swiftly as his clumsy dress would permit, he turned and sought the rack where the belts had been kept. It was empty. From it he made his way back to the door and, starting there, made a tour of the cabin, searching for the second lifebelt which should have been part of the equipment of the cabin.

Not that he expected to find it, but so startling was the suggestion which had entered his mind, that before he accepted it, even tentatively, he was determined to probe it to the bottom. The most careful searching failed to reveal it, and as the signals on the rope attached to his waist were now becoming urgent, proving the anxiety of those up above, he retraced his steps to the door and, with the kris in his hand, started back along the passage.

On his way he stopped once —at one of the other cabins. Stepping through the open doorway he made his way to the rack where the lifebelts were kept. A moment's examination showed him that two belts were in the rack and, on looking closer, he saw that the number of the cabin was stamped on each. Then he backed out and continued his way to the deck.

As he came out of the saloon entrance, and walked to the side, he at first did not see a dark shadow which hovered directly above him; but when, a moment later, he turned towards the bow he started back sharply. Poised over him, and regarding him with frightful intensity, was a long narrow shape, which moved slowly along.

Blake gazed at it in stupefaction. He had descended into those coral-lined depths, fully prepared to risk its dangers; but in their most terrible form, those dangers had not encompassed anything worse than the murderous blue shark.

Now above him he saw a menace which he knew instinctively was not a blue shark. Yet it had a strange resemblance to that savage creature, though it was fully three times as large. Suddenly the truth flashed upon him, and in the grip of realisation, he backed towards the saloon entrance.

He knew now that it was indeed a shark, but such a shark as man rarely encountered. It was the feared and terrible whale shark, inhabitant of those waters, and more savage than any other monster of the deep.

And what had Blake with which to meet it should it attack him? A hatchet in his belt and, clutched in his hand, the long bladed kris which he was certain had been the cause of Ferguson's death. He had read of the whale shark, he had studied its history, but never before had he seen it in its native element.

If the waters about him were its haunt, he was in a decidedly nasty position, for though he might seek temporary safety in the saloon, it would avail him little. The shark might remain at hand for hours.

And there was the frail air-tube which was the sole thread holding him to life. One gentle sweep of that great tail, and both air-tube and signalling cord would snap like thread. Then, indeed, would his position be desperate.

Blake's heart almost stopped for a moment as he saw the huge creature slowly turn and inspect the frail cords which held him to the life-giving air above. As its great body swept past them, he strained tensely, but evidently they were too insignificant for the shark to pay any attention to, for he passed them with contempt.

But not so the strange creature on the deck of the steamer. Never before had he seen such a "fish," and the attention which later might be turned to savage attack was now but wonderment. Probably he was trying to understand what Blake was, and why he had had the temerity to invade his haunts. At any rate, Blake realised that for the moment he was safe from attack.

He debated within himself whether to retain the position he held or attempt to reach the surface. Certainly, if the great whale shark rushed him, no amount of pulling from the yacht could help him to escape. Yet the air tube worried him greatly, and it was owing to it that he finally decided to risk an ascent.

Slowly he made his way to the rail, and was just about to signal to the yacht, when, with a great sweep of its tail which threatened to smash both cord and air-tube, the shark came towards him. Never in his life had Blake faced such a terrible crisis, and he knew it.

Ably as he might defend himself, no strength or strategy would avail him did the air-tube come within the orbit of the shark's course, and should such a calamity occur it meant a sure and speedy death — like a rat in a trap. Still, he held his ground firmly, and raising the kris which he had brought waited.

When still a few feet away from him the shark turned, and for a moment a wave of relief passed over Blake as he saw the creature swim away, but the relief swiftly changed to dismay as the shark again turned and made for him at an ever-increasing speed.

About his intentions there could now be no question. It was no doubt irritated at the strange creature which had invaded its haunts, and intending sweeping it from its path. On it came straight for Blake, and as its great bulk of two score feet overshadowed him he felt like a pigmy pitted against a mastodon of old. Yet he held his ground.

A single moment only the shark hesitated, then it turned slightly, and with the speed of an express train shot forwards. Watching his chance, Blake sprang to one side, and as the huge white body flashed past him buried the knife up to the hilt.

A great cloud of crimson gushed forth, changing the clear water to a muddy cloud, it was impossible to see what damage he had done, for the shark had swept on; but he did know that he had drawn blood, and that so far the air cord held.

As the blood-clouded water cleared somewhat he turned and saw the shark coming at him even swifter than before. The wound he had given it had roused it to a wild anger, and it was determined to sweep him from its path with one snap of its mighty jaws.

But the first meeting had served to steady Blake's nerves, and this time he took the kris in his left hand and drew the axe from his belt with the other. On the shark came like a bolt and just as it turned Blake repeated his former tactics.

A thrill went through him as he felt the head of the axe bury itself in the side of the shark, and instinctly he knew that the deep-sunk blade of the kris had found a mortal spot. The crimson wave which muddied the water was awful, and the sudden churning all about him told Blake that the shark was whirling madly, seeking for him.

Only chance enabled him to meet the creature's third rush, but luck was again with him. Twice he succeeded in thrusting in the kris to the hilt, but so deep did he bury the axe that it was carried away as the shark swept past.

Then the great creature simply went mad. Vaguely Blake was aware that it was darting back and forth in great death rushes, and each moment he expected the air-pipe to go or to feel himself swept within the vortex of its struggles.

That those on the yacht were aware that something serious was happening to him was evident, for the signals on the cord were urgent. But Blake was not yet prepared to risk an ascent through that troubled water, and a moment later his caution proved its wisdom, for through the clouded water came the shark in a fourth terrific rush.

With his knife poised, Blake awaited it, and when it got close to him stabbed again and again. Then he pulled frantically on the cord, signalling those on the yacht to draw him up. Only too willingly they responded, and up he went as fast as the winch could raise him.

It seemed ages before he shot up above the surface, and all during the ascent he expected to feel the swirl of the shark's rush. But he made the trip in safety, and when after being dragged over the side, and having the front plate of his helmet removed, he followed the outstretched arms of the others with his gaze he saw the reason why. The whale shark had come to the surface in its death struggles, and even now was crimsoning the water before them.

Not until the end of his life would Blake forget the appealing question in Yvonne's eyes as she bent over him and urged the sailors to assist him out of the diving suit. When the heavy helmet had been unscrewed he smiled up at her reassuringly.

"It is all right, Yvonne," he said. "I had a bit of a brush down below, but, fortunately, won out."

"A bit of a brush!" she cried, with swimming eyes. "Do you call a fight with that gigantic shark a bit of a brush? Do you call a struggle to the death with it a casual occurrence? Look at it floating on the water! Look at the crimson about it! It is almost unbelievable that you met it and killed it. We knew up here something terrible was happening to you, and when —when the first red came up we were afraid it —"

"There, I know," interrupted Blake soothingly. "I won't deny that for a little while it was touch and go, but it has ended all right."

But Yvonne would not be satisfied that he was quite all right until he finally stepped from the diving suit, and, with a hand as steady as a rock, lighted a cigarette. At that moment the rest of the party turned from their contemplation of the dead whale shark, and for some minutes Blake was forced to receive their congratulations.

Nothing would do Captain Vaughan but to send a boat to tow the shark alongside the yacht and to recover from its side the hatchet which Blake had buried there.

And here it may be mentioned that to this day the self-same axe hangs in Captain Vaughan's cabin on the Fleur-de-Lys, a prized memento of Blake's great struggle, and bearing on the blade an inscription relating the particulars, date and place of the fight, and when it is considered that the whale shark measured exactly thirty-six feet[1] the true magnitude of the feat may be realised.

Before being permitted to tell his tale Blake was forced to submit to three ringing cheers from the admiring sailors of the yacht, led by Hendricks, his old enemy; then, with Captain Lamport holding his arm, he moved to the promenade aft there to report on what he had seen.

As he seated himself he glanced at the eager circle with a smile.

"I know you are all most anxious to know what I discovered, so I will be brief. To begin with, Captain Lamport, I found the Kara Maru without much difficulty. She went down here all right, and an examination of the stern proved that the sole survivor told the truth about the propeller. It had certainly been lost before she struck.

---

[1] The little known whale shark of the Pacific sometimes reaches a length of fifty feet. —
EDITOR.

"She lies in about seventeen fathoms, and is held from going deeper by a small coral valley. And she is almost on even keel; it was not difficult for me to get aboard. I made my way to Cabin 20, and on arriving there found your anticipations realised. Poor Ferguson was in his bunk when she went down."

"And the pearl —the crimson pearl?" exclaimed Captain Lamport eagerly. "You got it?"

Blake shook his head.

"No," he said quietly. "I did not get it because it wasn't there. Someone has been before me."

"Wasn't there! Someone had been before you! Then that means, Mr. Blake, that it has been secured by the Chinese on the junk! We must go after them at once."

Blake held up his hand.

"Wait, Captain Lamport. I said someone had been before me, but I am not at all convinced that the pearl was secured by the Chinese on the junk.

"In the first place, Ferguson lost the pearl just before the Kara Maru foundered, and, moreover, I may tell you that he did not meet his death by drowning. He was murdered before the ship struck, and the pearl was torn from his neck then."

The captain leaned back weakly, while the others regarded Blake with puzzled glances.

"I know this seems difficult to believe," he went on, "but I will tell you what I saw, and the theory I have since built up. In the first place, Ferguson was murdered. I am not sure yet who did it, but certainly a Chinaman was mixed up in it.

"On reaching Cabin 20 the first thing I discovered, was the body of a Chinaman on the floor. He had been held down by some things that had fallen over when the ship struck. Beside him was this kris — the same, by the way, which saved my life when I was attacked by the shark.

"I thought his being there was queer, but when I found Ferguson I saw that it was no coincidence. Ferguson had been stabbed in the heart, and the pouch containing the pearl torn from his neck.

"Now, my first thought was that the Chinaman on the floor had murdered him, and had gained possession of the pearl, but had been caught by the foundering of the ship. A search of him showed that it was not on him, however, and an examination of Ferguson's clothes showed that he had nothing whatsoever in them.

"I jumped to the conclusion that San, the Chinaman in charge of the junk, had found the pearl in the possession of his fellow, and had brought it away with him. But just as I was leaving something happened which caused my mind to shoot back to an incident which, when it happened, appeared trivial. And the more I think of it the more I am certain my ideas must be readjusted.

"In order, however, that my mind alone may not be the sole judge I am going to ask Tinker a question. Tinker, do you remember the lifebelt which was left on the beach by the sailors from the schooner after they had brought ashore the survivor from the Kara Maru?"

"You mean the brown one we saw when we came back from the bush, guv'nor?"

"Yes."

"Yes, sir, I remember it."

"Do you remember if it had anything stamped on it?"

"Yes, sir, it did."

"And do you recollect what it was?"

"It was —oh, I see what you are driving at, guv'nor! It was the number twenty."

"Exactly! Now to proceed. As I said, when I noticed that number on the lifebelt which had been left on the beach I attached no importance to it. But now it assumes a vast meaning in my eyes.

"To explain. I said something had happened just as I was about to leave the cabin. I felt a touch on my shoulder, and, turning, discovered there was a lifebelt drifting about the cabin. I drew it round in front of me, and more by accident than design noticed that it was stamped with the number twenty.

"I at once recollected that was the number of the cabin in which I stood, and knew the lifebelt was part of its equipment. It was then that my mind shot back to an exactly similar lifebelt which I had seen on the beach, and when I realised that not only was it a duplicate, but had the same number stamped upon it as well I got something of a shock.

"I made my way to the rack where they had been kept, but there was nothing there. Then I searched the cabin thoroughly, but could not find a second. Yet I knew there should have been a second if none of the occupants of the cabin had escaped. I moved along then to another cabin where the occupants had been caught as the ship went down, and there in the rack were two lifebelts."

A deep sigh which ran round the circle showed how deep was the interest in Blake's story, but none interrupted him. They were too anxious to hear the rest.

Presently he continued.

"Now, to get straight to the matter in hand, this seems, to my mind, to be the situation. Ferguson shipped on the Kara Maru, and when she was being driven off her course was in his cabin. Just before she struck, a Chinaman —we may even suspect him of being one of the Celestials whom Captain Lamport thinks was after the pearl — entered the cabin and killed him.

"At this point we come to two theories, each of which seems plausible enough. The first is this: The Chinaman, after getting possession of the pearl, may have been caught when the ship foundered, and drowned beside his victim. Then when the junk arrived, and San descended, he may have found the pearl and secured it. If that is the case, he has it now.

"The second theory is this. A lifebelt stamped with the number twenty has been found on the beach here. We know it was used by the only man who escaped from the wreck. Where there should be two lifebelts in Ferguson's cabin there is now only one.

"Therefore, it seems a reasonable theory that the man who survived used one of the lifebelts belonging to cabin twenty. If that is so he must have been in there just before the ship struck.

"Did he arrive after Ferguson was killed? Or did he go there as an accomplice of the Chinaman? We don't know. Did he have a struggle with the Chinaman for the possession of the pearl, and, leaving the other there, escape? Or did he arrive just in time to snatch the pearl, secure a lifebelt, and make his way to the deck?

"We don't know that, but a struggle between him and the Chinaman does not seem to have been an impossibility, for the Chinaman still bears the mark of a nasty wound on his forehead.

"Supposing this man who survived the wreck did gain possession of the pearl? Then he still has it, and, instead of being beneath the sea or on the junk, it is on board the schooner which was stolen by Black McCabe and this man.

"And let us consider something else. This man who survived had much to be grateful for to Johnson, the trader. Yet we see him here when Black McCabe shot the trader, and we see him joining forces with McCabe to raid the schooner and sail away in her.

"Now that alone proves he is not a man of the proper calibre. If he were he would have secured McCabe and held him. Instead, however, he turns pirate with him. But one thing we have been told, and that is his name. It was William Carr, and he was apparently a seaman in the Kara Maru."

Suddenly Captain Vaughan's voice broke in.

"William Carr!" he exclaimed. "I had a William Carr sailing with me at one time. He was a Yankee —a harmless little fellow and as honest as the day. He would never turn pirate."

"That description doesn't fit the man who was saved from the Kara Maru," said Blake. "He seems to have been a big, bearded man —quite a different type entirely. But he also claimed to be a Yankee.

"It is an odd coincidence to find two men of that name sailing in these waters, for it is not a common name. In fact, so odd it is that I am inclined to think that, when the matter is investigated, we will find a flaw in the tale. However, that but strengthens the second theory I have outlined.

"At any rate, there are the two theories, Captain Lamport. Both are fairly plausible. Both may be wrong —both can't be right. One of them may be, however, and in the absence of any others it seems as though one of them should be selected and considered. Now which do you favour?"

"Well, Mr. Blake, when you outlined the first one I felt that it must be the correct one. But when you went on to the second I began to feel it sounded more like what had happened. Balancing the two, however, I am inclined to lean towards the first one, though, mind you, that bit about the lifebelt is hard to get over. But what do you think yourself?"

Before answering Blake lighted a fresh cigarette, then he rose.

"I will tell you which one I think is the right one," he said quietly. "I think the pearl is not beneath the sea, and I think it is not on board the junk. I do think it is on board the schooner which was stolen, and that the sole survivor of the Kara Maru is in possession of it.

"And something which strengthens me in my opinion is this. Were the crimson pearl on board the junk it is a certainty that she would be getting away from this spot as fast as her clumsy sails would carry her. But is she? No. Cast your eyes over the side, captain. What do you see?"

"By heavens, Mr. Blake, it is the junk!"

"Nothing else. She is much closer than she was an hour ago, which proves that the pearl is not aboard her, and that they are but beating about, waiting for us to get out of the way. San the wily, San the cunning, thinks the pearl is still on the Kara Maru."

"Then that means what, Mr. Blake?"

"It means, captain, that if you wish to regain possession of your pearl you must find the survivor of the Kara Maru —the man who gave the name of William Carr, and who, in company with Black McCabe, the man I am after, stole my chartered schooner, the Eastern Queen, and escaped in her.

"It seems that our paths run parallel, so, since it is to our mutual interests to find that schooner, and, as I certainly intend to do so if I have to spend the rest of my life at it, I think the best thing we can do is to discuss our plans and act without delay."

BLAKE'S
GREAT
FIGHT
IN THE
DEEP. .

A single moment only the shark hesitated, then it turned, and with the speed of an express train shot forward.

U. J.—No. 564.

WHEN its small size and meagre population is considered, Thursday Island is a more than ordinarily important spot in the East. In appearance it is not unlike the other coral islands which abound in those waters, and certainly in itself there is nothing maddeningly attractive to the traveller.

It is an insignificant member of an insignificant archipelago situated at the very apex of York Peninsula —the northernmost point of Australia. Were it not for the fact that pearl fishing abounds there it might still be but a name on the map. But as always, when the prospect of gain is the lure, there are many men to follow its beckoning finger. And so it is with Thursday Island.

Almost the only thing which gives it a claim to rank as a place of residence is its pearl fishing, and in pursuit of the elusive pearl there foregather at Thursday Island about as motley and adventurous a crew of individuals as it is possible to find in the East.

There are white men from every European country —most of them frankly adventurers, some of them besotten dregs of civilisation who have touched there for the time in their eternal drifting about the world —Chinese, Cingalese, Japanese, Javanese, Kanakas, and what not. And the sole aim of each and everyone of them is the pearl.

The whites and Chinese to finance, the Japs to dive and steal, the Kanakas and others to thrust their ugly faces in where opportunity offers. So goes the round of life in that small tropical island dignified by the name of a day of the week.

In the laying out of the settlement itself neither rhyme nor reason was used. It is but a hotch-potch conglomeration of shacks and buildings which, as is always the case when the Celestial element predominates, reeks with dark suggestion and mystery when the blackness of night enshrouds them.

What mysterious disappearances and undiscovered crimes have taken place there no man can tell. They are wrapped in the silence of the Orient, and only the cause is known —the lure of pearl. Many men have found that for which they sought —a peerless gem from the deep.

By that mysterious way in which the Celestial seems to know all that goes on the man has been marked down. If the lure of the gambling den or the drinking inferno fail to bring him within their toils, then sterner measures are adopted.

A moonless night, the shadow of the palm groves, a bared blade, and the deed is done. One more human being goes to join the great mass who have gone before, and another pearl is added to the hoard of some slant-eyed Celestial.

And to this haunt of Oriental stealth and greed there came one day a small boat bearing two men; where they came from they said not, nor did any question. How they came to be in those treacherous waters in such a frail craft was their own secret, and none sought to discover it.

A few may have remarked the fact that the name of the tiny boat had been scraped off, and more could have told you it was of the type carried by the schooners which traded amongst the islands.

But what name may have been painted upon it, or to what schooner it may have belonged, none knew, and the two men who came in it did not offer to explain. Personal questions are not a part of the island etiquette.

In appearance the two men were not unlike the average bearded adventurers who throng the East. Both were dark and hirsute, but there the resemblance between them ended. The taller of the two was truly a commanding figure, and, thick though his beard was, it did not hide the powerful sweep of the jaw beneath.

He was dressed in thin, ragged clothes stained and shapeless from exposure, but even they failed to conceal the supple lines of the mighty frame.

Above the beard a pair of deep, intelligent eyes peered forth, and when taken in conjunction with the finely-shaped head and long thin hands, they gave the finishing touch to a more than ordinary personality. And indeed it was, for the stranger was Rymer. The other was Black McCabe —brutally coarse beside Rymer.

How they had reached Thursday Island in a small open boat is a brief tale. After leaving Rubilinga they had, by the aid of the four Kanakas, worked the schooner Eastern Queen in a Westerly direction until they had entered Torres Strait —that narrow, treacherous ribbon of water which separates the northern point of Australia from Papua.

There she was brought up, and preparations made to leave her. While McCabe had provisioned the boat Rymer had called the Kanakas together. Ever since his masterly stroke back in the lagoon they had stood in complete awe of him, and when he had curtly bade them work the schooner back to Rubilinga he knew they would obey.

The unfortunate seaman who had been cast into the hold had been kept prisoner during the trip, and Rymer forbade the Kanakas to release him until the small boat was out of sight. He knew, even though he were not there, that they would follow his orders to the letter. Then the small boat had been launched, and, together with McCabe, he set out across the strait for Thursday Island. And now they had arrived safely.

Their coming to this island in preference to adopting some other plan was due to Rymer. The question had been argued hotly between him and McCabe, but the stronger will of Rymer had triumphed.

McCabe had favoured a long sail north until they reached Hong Kong, but Rymer, realising to the full what the piracy of the Eastern Queen meant, desired to get rid of her as quickly as possible.

At the same time it was necessary that they should choose a lawless spot where gentlemen of their kidney might pass unchallenged. Port Moresby had been considered, and certainly the great unknown bush behind it was strongly in its favour.

Had it been simply a question of eluding capture there is no doubt but that Rymer would have chosen it. But he knew the chase after him was not of the same description as the pursuit of McCabe, and, with financial resources behind him, he had no doubt that he could soon lose himself in one of the great capitals of Europe or the East.

Not for some time had he held so much concentrated wealth in his possession as was contained in that flaming pearl he had secured. Not even McCabe knew he possessed it, nor did Rymer intend he should.

His one idea was to turn it into more negotiable wealth as quickly as possible, for he knew it would not be long before divers would be at work upon the Kara Maru. He realised, moreover, that there would be a hue and cry tor the solitary survivor, and he had no wish for the limelight.

He did not care a rap what became of McCabe. The lesser crook had served his purpose, and already Rymer was planning to "shake" him, realising the extra danger of being in the company of a man who was wanted as badly as was McCabe.

And it was at Thursday Island that Rymer felt he could get rid of his pearl at a fat price. Not that it would be easy. Every Chinaman in the place would covet it, and more than one would quickly enter into negotiations for its purchase. But where one would deal on the level a dozen would sit up nights racking their cunning brains for some plan to get possession of it.

Once it was known that Rymer had it he would carry his life in his hands, and none knew that better than he. Nevertheless, he reckoned on his own shrewdness to outwit those who would try to bring him down, and, in a long career of adventurous crime, he had a fair estimate of his own abilities.

Little did McCabe realise the mental workings of his partner.

He was too exercised over his own position to pay much attention to Rymer. His sole idea was to get rid of the swag he carried, and with the proceeds to seek out some spot in the East where he could drop out of sight until the thing blew over.

Unfortunately he did not know of the vow made by Sexton Blake by which the latter had sworn to remain on the trail until he had put Black McCabe where he belonged.

Before putting into effect any of his own plans, Rymer led the way to a low verandah shack, which was locally known as the hotel, though it served more as a drinking centre for the toughest specimens of the place than for any other purpose.

From the bearded brigand who owned it Rymer secured one of the few dirty rooms it possessed, and to this he and McCabe made their way at once. No sooner had they entered than Rymer locked the door and drew McCabe into the middle of the room.

"Now, look here, Black," he said, in low, inaudible tones, "we have reached the point where something must be done to guard against the future. So far we have played in luck, but you know as well as I do that it is only a matter of time before the schooner is sighted.

"If the Kanakas do succeed in working her back to Rubilinga then you can bet all you got in London that Blake will be on our heels. Not that I would mind coming to grips with him out here, but, as I told you, I am on a good thing, and publicity is just what I don't want.

"I don't think he has the ghost of a notion that I am in this part of the world, and I don't want him to. On the other hand he must be after you in dead earnest. I know him well enough to know that only a big thing would bring him out here and cause him to risk an expedition into the bush as he did.

"So it stands to reason he is not going to give up yet. That means, that so long as I am with you, I increase the danger to myself. But I have benefited by the partnership so far, and I am willing to continue it until we are both out of danger. But if I do it must be on two conditions."

"What are they?" grunted McCabe.

"These. Firstly, that you get rid of your swag here in Thursday Island, and secondly, that you submit to my ruling. As far as I can see you increase your danger just about one hundred per cent, by sticking to the swag.

"The secret of success in our game is to keep every haul changing hands as much as possible. That covers the trail, and often succeeds in breaking the pursuit entirely."

"I'm willing enough to get rid of the stuff," responded McCabe. "I tried to in Cape Town, but the fence there wanted it for next to nothing. It cost me a lot, and I'm hanged if I am going to give it away."

"That won't be necessary. This joint is full of Chinks, and every one of them will deal with you. It is a cinch for them. They will pay you at least half the value and get rid of it in Hong Kong or Shanghai. At any rate, if you stay with me until we are clear you must do it; I intend getting rid of my stuff here."

"Your stuff!" exclaimed McCabe. "What have you got? I knew you were on to a good thing, but I did not know you had any swag to get rid of. It must be mighty small if you carry it with you."

"Never you mind what it is," answered Rymer curtly. "I haven't displayed any curiosity about your stuff, and don't propose telling you about mine.

"But to get back to business. I am going out now to look up Charlie Wong. He is one of the wealthiest, and at the same time, one of the safest Chinks here. He runs a big gambling joint and knows everything that is happening from Hong Kong to Sydney and from Batavia to Tahiti.

"I'll try and get him to handle your stuff as well as mine if you wish."

"All right. What will I do in the meantime?"

"Stay here in this room. If you drink have it sent in. Say you have a fever —say anything excuse for not going out. And let me tell you for your own good, Black, if you want to get any benefit out of your swag, watch it every second. There isn't a man out there who wouldn't slit you open for it. I shall not be long."

With that Rymer turned and made his way out of the room. He went straight past the bar and out into the sandy street, which was lined with a sufficient number of shacks to give it the semblance of a main thoroughfare.

At the moment the street was almost deserted, for it was early afternoon, and the tropical sun was beating fiercely down. But Rymer seemed not to mind it, for he stepped out briskly and headed down the street towards a long, low-lying building which bore a sign informing the world —or that portion of it which touched at Thursday Island — that it was Charlie Wong's General Emporium.

In order to justify its name it exhibited in the two small window recesses an assortment of articles which ranged from stringed onions to cotton shirts and trousers, but if Charlie Wong had depended on the trading end of his establishment he would have amassed little.

It was of small importance to Charlie Wong, however, being but the blind with which the Celestial believes in cloaking his real business. And in the back of the building was established one part of the Chinaman's serious pursuits. That was the gambling room, known to every man in Thursday Island.

It was plainly but comfortably furnished for that part of the world. At one end was a bar, which, when the evening game was on, did a rushing business.

Then it took two half naked Kanaka boys to serve the drinks as quickly as the impatient customers demanded them, but, with all the amount which flowed, the man was yet to be found who was permitted too much at the tables.

Not that Charlie Wong had any moral scruples. On the contrary. But when a man reached that stage, one of two things happened. If the Chink knew his pockets to be empty he was unceremoniously thrown out to recover as best he could.

If he were possessed of anything worth taking, then he was shown into a private room where he could drink his fill, and from which he usually emerged as thoroughly stripped as the artistic Celestial could strip him.

And more than once it had happened that men had entered those private rooms never to emerge. What had occurred to them nobody knew. Once, a man, brave with the bravery born of alcohol, had publicly accused Charlie Wong of being the cause of a man's disappearance.

Charlie Wong had listened to the accusation with his wide, sickly smile, and did not even reply. But the next morning that same man was found on the beach with his throat cut. After that no more accusations were made against Charlie Wong.

Nor was the gambling room, and the opportunities it provided for pickings, the only source of Charlie's income. It was rumoured that many pearling floats were financed by him, and in some mysterious way it seemed to be taken for granted that he had amassed a big fortune out of them.

But what only the underworld of that place knew was that Charlie Wong would buy anything marketable and ask no questions. To him went the Jap divers with their stolen pearls; to him went the Kanakas with their scrapings; to him went the great proportion of the human vultures who snatched what they could.

And in this part of his business did Charlie Wong act with a far-sighted fairness. It would have been easy for him to outpoint the thieves who came to him with their booty.

None, however, realised better than the long-headed Celestial that a comparatively fair deal with his clients of the underworld meant more money in the long run to him. By such treatment they would always seek him, and only Charlie Wong knew where all the stuff he secured went and what was his profit on it.

To this place it was that Rymer made his way. Passing through the front part where the trade goods were displayed he sought the back room. Very few people were there, for not until evening would the real gaming begin. Half a dozen of the habitues, however, were gathered about, some of them staking at a faro game which was in progress, and others playing a desultory game of poker.

Charlie Wong himself was not to be seen, so, passing the small group of gamblers, Rymer strode to the bar, behind which stood a Chinaman.

"Whisky and soda," he ordered curtly.

When the man had pushed the bottle across Rymer poured his drink, and after a deep swallow beckoned the man closer.

"Where is Charlie?" he asked in low voiced Chinese.

The Celestial shrugged.

"I don't know," he answered, eyeing Rymer under heavy lids.

"Look here," snapped Rymer bending forward and fixing his eyes on those of the other. "I want to see Charlie at once. Do you get me? You get out from behind that bar and tell him, or I will throw you out. See! Now move."

The Celestial's movements could hardly be called brisk, but in compliance with Rymer's threatening order he did move away, and coming out from behind the bar disappeared through a door at the far end of the gambling room.

While he was gone Rymer sipped leisurely at his drink, and had just finished it when the Celestial came back.

"You come with me," he said in English. "Charlie see you."

With a curt nod Rymer followed him to the door at the end, and, passing through, found himself in a narrow passage off which opened several rooms. Into one of these his guide showed him, and closing the door left him alone.

The room was small and barely furnished. A table, half a dozen chairs and a couch comprised its contents. It was windowless, an oil lamp suspended from the ceiling supplying the necessary illumination.

Rymer sat down on the edge of the couch and drummed irritably on his knee for some minutes. He was suddenly roused by a soft click to his right, and turning sharply, saw a stout Chinaman standing at his elbow.

Now the door was on Rymer's left, and from where he sat it was in his line of vision. He knew, therefore, that the Celestial before him had not come that way. Instinctively he realised that somewhere in the evenly panelled wall was a secret door, and by it the other had made his entry.

It was but in keeping with the mysterious atmosphere of the whole place, and served to make Rymer realise that he was up against brains as cunning as the East could produce.

He rose at once and stood leaning against the table.

"Well, Charlie Wong," he said. "I don't suppose you will remember me. It is several years since we met in —Canton."

Wong, for it was he, advanced a step, and examined Rymer's features critically, then he nodded slowly.

"I remember you. Why have you sought me out?"

"To do business," responded Rymer briefly. "When I knew you last you were always ready to turn a trick, Charlie, and I don't suppose you have changed with the years."

"I have not changed," replied the Celestial evenly. "What have you to dispose of?"

Rymer drew up a chair and sat down, motioning the Chinaman to do likewise. When he had done so Rymer leaned forward.

"Before I tell you what I possess," he said quietly. "I want to ask you a question."

"Well."

"Can you handle a deal which will take, at least, a hundred thousand pounds?"

For a moment the Celestial's eyes closed, then he looked up.

"It is a lot of money, but I could get it —yes, if the stuff is not bulky."

"It is not. You could put it in a cigarette."

"It is then?"

"A stone."

"What kind?"

"A pearl —the most wonderful pearl that ever came from the sea."

"Have you it with you?"

"No!" lied Rymer. "Do you think I am mad to carry a thing like that in here with me. But I can get it when necessary."

"It must be a remarkable pearl to be worth that much."

"It is worth double that, and when you see it you will say so."

"Can you describe it? Perhaps you are mistaken in its value. We get some fine pearls here, but never one which is worth that amount."

Rymer shrugged.

"I tell you I know its value," he said curtly. "I haven't handled stones all my life for nothing. It is not large, but a perfect specimen, and inside is something which makes it, as far as I know, the only one of its kind.

"That something is a crimson glow which, when you hold the pearl close, seems like living flame. Wait until you see it. It is worth anything, and if you buy at the figure I named, you will double your money."

While Rymer had been talking, the Celestial had been sitting with lowered lids, as though utterly indifferent to the wonders of the priceless gem the other was describing; but when Rymer spoke of the crimson glow which pervaded it, not even Wong's Oriental control could keep from his eyes the sudden flash which appeared in them.

Lucky it was for him that his lids veiled that flash from Rymer. In a moment it was gone again, and when he looked up, Rymer never dreamed that he had just described something which had already been the cause of much thought on the part of Charlie Wong.

His voice was as toneless and even as ever.

"This pearl," he said. "Where did you get it?"

"Never mind that. I have it, and nobody knows it is in my possession. Its existence is known to only a few people, and they think it is at the bottom of the sea. It is the safest deal you ever tackled, Charlie."

For a few moments there was silence, while the inscrutable eyes of the Celestial rested on the table. Finally he looked up.

"I tell you," he said, "I can't raise that money alone, but I know a man who might put it up. He is not in Thursday Island just now, but I expect him at any moment. You hang about here until he comes, then if he wants the pearl we can make a deal."

"All right, Charlie, that suits me," said Rymer, as he rose. "By the way, there is a man with me, Charlie, who has a nice bunch of stuff which he wants to get rid of. I will bring him in to-night. He can tell you what it is, and you can make a deal with him as well. It is bulky, but worth getting."

"You bring him in, and I will talk with him," answered the Celestial non-committally.

With a nod Rymer turned and made for the door. When it had closed after him, Charlie Wong stood motionless until his footsteps had died away down the passage.

Not until he heard the distant slam of the door leading into the gaming-room did he move. Then he sat down at the table and drew out a yellow cigarette. When it was lighted he leaned back and closed his eyes.

"So, so," he muttered softly. "San is on a wild-goose chase. Instead of being at the bottom of the sea in the Kara Maru, the pearl is in the possession of the man who has just left. What does it all mean?

"The report that the Kara Maru went down off Rubilinga was straight enough, and it was reported that only one man escaped. Both my agents went down on her, and San hoped a diver would locate the pearl on the body of Ferguson.

"But now this man Rymer, one of the cleverest crooks living, drops into this place as casually as though to pass the time of day, and calmly talks about a crimson pearl.

"It is not possible that there can be two such pearls in the world. Then the pearl he has must be the one we thought on the Kara Maru. It is possible that Rymer got possession of it at Brisbane, and that Ferguson did not have it with him when the ship went down?

"That seems most likely. Else how did he get it? It is hardly likely that he is the one whom is mentioned as being the only survivor. But I must find out how he got here, then to send word to San at once."

Charlie Wong rose as he reached this point in his meditations, and approaching the panelled wall, pressed his fingers against a spot high up. Instantly one of the panels opened, revealing a black void on the other side.

The Celestial stepped through at once, closing the panel after him. Now he was in utter darkness, but he was evidently familiar with his surroundings, for, guided by the wall, he walked ahead confidently until he brought up against another wall straight ahead of him.

Passing his fingers along it, he pressed again, and as a panel here slid back, he stepped through the opening into one of the most luxuriously-furnished rooms in a prodigal East.

It was Wong's sanctum sanctorum, and displayed in its Oriental richness the man's taste. The walls were draped with heavy silken hangings of gold and crimson, the floor obscured by rich Eastern rugs, the ceiling decorated with a medley of Chinese scenes, and all about the place were low divans piled high with rich cushions.

At the far end was a heavy teakwood desk, over which was suspended a great copper lamp, and it was towards this desk that Charlie Wong made his way. Seating himself in the huge chair, which matched the massive lines of the desk, he leaned forward as any European business man might have done, and pressed one of several buttons set in a bed of ebony.

Almost at once the curtains in one corner parted, and a slim Chinese youth appeared. He bowed low before his master and waited.

"Find out for me what you can about the bearded man who just left me," said Wong curtly.

"Oh, illustrious one, my worthless ears have already heard what is known!" replied the youth in liquid accents.

"Speak!" commanded Wong.

"But to-day, illustrious one, he with another came. A small open boat brought them. It had borne a name, but that had been removed, and where they came from none can tell. They went at once to the hotel, where one remained while the other came here."

"That is all?"

"It is all my worthless ears have heard, illustrious one, and it is all that is known."

"Go at once and tell Foo to come here."

"I hasten to obey, illustrious one."

With that the youth disappeared, as silently as he had come. When the curtains had dropped behind him, Wong opened a long, shallow drawer in the desk and took out a large chart. Spreading it out before him, he began studying it, and any sea captain could have told you it was a chart of the South Pacific.

Slowly the Celestial traced a line from Thursday Island to a small spot in the Solomons. After that he made several calculations, and had just finished when the curtains once more parted and another Chinaman entered.

This one was a big, weather-beaten individual, who had the stamp of the sea upon him, and Charlie Wong's first words proved that to be so.

"Captain," he said curtly, "you are ready to put to sea?"

"Yes, illustrious one."

"Engines and crew ready?"

The other bowed.

"Come here!" commanded Wong.

Captain Foo approached the desk and stood waiting.

"I want you to take the launch and put to sea at once. On the chart here I have marked the course you are to take and your destination. Follow that closely. You are going in order to find his Excellency and bring him back. I will give you a letter to him.

"If you do not meet him on your way, keep on to the island. If he is not there, return. But remember this. I want him to return urgently. That is all. I will send the letter to you in a few minutes."

"It shall be done, illustrious one," answered the captain, and with a low bow he departed.

When once more alone, Charlie Wong drew out a piece of paper, and began to compose the letter which would bring San hastening back to Thursday Island in the speedy steam-launch which he was sending.

And at the same moment two other things which bore on the course of events were transpiring. One was a remark which Rymer was making to Black McCabe. It was:

"So you see, Black, what I have arranged. To-night you come down to Charlie Wong's joint with me, and we will fix up about your stuff. Then, when his principal returns, I will finish up my business, and after that we will shake the dust of this place off our feet, and beat it for Hong Kong or Manila."

The other thing was a slim, graceful steam-yacht which was just approaching the island. And on her stern was the name Fleur-de-Lys.

THE ELEVENTH CHAPTER. *Blake and Rymer Meet.*

THE events which transpired between the time when Blake made his startling discovery on the sunken Kara Maru, and when the Fleur-de-Lys reached Thursday Island, will stand for always as an example of the man's dynamic energy in full blast.

No sooner had he outlined his theory regarding the whereabouts of the crimson pearl, than he was unanimously chosen to take charge of matters and make whatever move he thought best.

The speedy Fleur-de-Lys was placed at his disposal, together with Captain Vaughan, Hendricks, and her doughty crew. More than once in the past had Blake been ranged with, as well as against, Yvonne's sailors, and he knew to the finest point just how valuable they were. Besides, they were spoiling for a fight, and if future events should lead to such eventuality, Blake knew he could count on them to the last man.

As for Yvonne herself, when she found Blake was really to make the yacht his home for a time, her lips parted in a soft smile of happiness, and her eyes grew dreamy with secret joy. It was enough for her to know that once more the wheel of Fate had brought them together —that wheel which seemed to link their lives so strangely.

Captain Lamport, harassed with worry and disappointed over the result of Blake's descent into the sea, was only too glad to have his burden shifted on to the latter's able shoulders, and to have it incorporated with the puzzle at which Blake's mind was working.

So, once this decision was arrived at, Blake moved with almost bewildering rapidity. First he took Ford, the seaman from the stolen Eastern Queen, and, accompanied by Tinker, returned to the island. They found Captain Weeks feeling better, and when he heard Blake intended to move him to the yacht, he acquiesced rapidly.

With Abonga's assistance Ford got him down to the beach and settled into the boat. Next their few remaining belongings were carried down, and when the last article had been stowed away, Blake turned his attention to the blacks.

He realised full well what a risk it was to leave the savages alone without the moral restraint of a white man, but there was nothing else to be done. He had devoted more than a little thought to that same question, and had arrived to what he hoped would be a solution.

As it eventually turned out, it was a master stroke on his part. Not for nothing had he impressed the savages with his daring march into the bush.

Nor had the perils of the march and the great fight in the hill village lost anything in the relation by Abonga and the carriers who had accompanied him.

Moreover, the blacks had been forcibly influenced by his management of affairs since the death of the trader. He had met their first treachery by a cool bravery which had won out, and from that moment had controlled them.

Therefore they were in a state of mind towards him which made them receptive of his commands. This was what he hoped but could not tell.

Summoning them to the beach, he lined them up and began to address them. After referring sternly to the looting which had taken place after the trader's death, he touched on the murderous attack which had been made upon himself. Then he went on:

"The day has gone when you can do these things and not be punished. It will do you no good to hate the white man and seek to injure him. He will always triumph over you. But if you follow him, and work with him, you will profit.

"Let not the actions of one incur your enmity against all. Work in harmony with him, and you will be happier. The things you should not do he will not permit you to do, and if you do them you will be punished.

"What will be done about the burning and looting of the trading-station, I do not know. That rests with the Government; but remember this, if, while you are here alone, you do anything else of a similar nature, you will pay heavily for it.

"Another man will be here soon to rebuild and restock the store. Meet him with friendship when he comes. Until then, go on with the work I have started you doing. Show him that you have made an attempt to rebuild that which you have destroyed.

"I may even return myself, and if I do, I don't want to be disappointed. If you do this, your punishment for that which you have done will be less heavy.

"And now, before I leave, I am going to appoint one as your chief. That man is to be Abonga. To him I look to wield the authority I have wielded. To you I look for obedience. That is all."

A dead silence followed Blake's words until he turned, and, taking Abonga's hand, led him forward.

"This is your leader," he said sternly. "Obey him."

Then he turned and moved towards the boat, and, white man though he was, in all that crowd of savage cannibals, not a single unfriendly glance followed him.

As the boat pushed off, he looked back and saw Abonga haranguing his fellows earnestly. And not until long after did Blake hear that, with the exception of very few backslidings, the blacks conducted themselves with remarkable restraint until the arrival of the man who was to re-open the trading-station.

On arriving at the yacht, Captain Vaughan at once took charge of his brother captain, and the seaman was berthed forward with the crew. Then, just as they were sitting down to dinner, in the sumptuous saloon, the anchor was weighed, and the Fleur-de-Lys, with a dainty curtsey to the rolling, purple waves, set off through the starlit night for Port Moresby.

Two days later, after steaming at full speed, they entered the Straits, and, no sooner had they done so, then the look-out sighted a sail on the port bow. Through the glasses they made out her signals, and when Captain Vaughan saw the inserted ensign, he changed his course, and made towards her.

"Something wrong with her," he said, handing the glasses to Captain Weeks, who was now well enough to be about.

The latter took them, and gazed at the distant ship for a moment, then he gave a shout which brought Blake, Yvonne, and Tinker racing up from the after-deck. With shaking finger he pointed across the blue water.

"There she is! There she is!" he cried. "The Eastern Queen — my ship. Those scoundrels have either abandoned her or have run short of provisions. She is flying the distress signal."

Blake reached for the glasses, and trained them on the other ship. For a few moments he held them thus, then lowered them, and handed them to Yvonne.

"You are right, Captain Weeks," he said quietly. "It is the Eastern Queen. How long will it take to reach her?" he asked, turning to Captain Vaughan.

"We will be within hailing distance in twenty minutes," answered the latter.

Then all hands stood watching while the Fleur-de-Lys ramped over the blue water towards the distant sail, and, true to his word, Captain Vaughan had her within hailing distance in twenty minutes.

The sailor who had suffered so summarily at the hands of Rymer and Black McCabe, was on the poop, and at the wheel were two of the Kanakas. The other two were leaning over the rail.

The Fleur-de-Lys was run close, and when his voice could be heard, the white seaman shouted out the tale of what had befallen, and how the ship had been abandoned in the Straits. In less than ten minutes a boat had been lowered from the yacht, with Blake, Captain Weeks, the seaman Ford, and a party of Yvonne's sailors in her.

When they reached the Eastern Queen, Blake heard the tale with all its details. Then and there he held an impromptu council of war on the poop-deck. Both the Kanakas and the white seaman were of the opinion that the two pirates had made in the direction of Thursday Island instead of Port Moresby, and, influenced by this, Blake decided to try the former place

It was finally arranged that Captain Weeks was to remain on board, that he would keep Ford also, and thus, with the usual complement of the Eastern Queen, he prepared to navigate her. A load of supplies was brought over from the yacht, and with the understanding that she should change her course and follow the yacht to Thursday Island, Blake returned.

Then the Fleur-de-Lys got under way again, and with a waving of hands, started for her new destination. The following afternoon she raised the island, and that was how it came that just as Charlie Wong was writing an urgent letter to San, the yacht was gliding gently shorewards.

Yet a thing there was of which not only Charlie Wong was ignorant, but of which Rymer and McCabe and Blake were ignorant as well. That was the fact that San, who was beginning to loom so importantly in the strange network of intrigue which had been woven, was already on his way to Thursday Island.

Through powerful glasses he had watched the descent of a diver to the sunken Kara Maru, and, fearful lest another had sought and found the prize for which he had come, he had abandoned his own attempt in order to follow the yacht, determined to assure himself of the truth. Though a slow sailer, the junk had had a fair wind, and was much nearer the island than anyone guessed.

Now that he had reached the place where he hoped finally to come up with his quarry and end the long chase, Blake realised the utmost caution was necessary. While fully aware that Black McCabe would be on his guard, he had a very fair idea of the limits of that gentleman's mentality.

Not from McCabe did he expect any deeply subtle move. The crook's whole actions had been those of blind flight with little strategy, and only his tremendous start had permitted him to keep the lead so long. Not a single move he had made had indicated daring or shrewdness in his nature, and in no way could Blake credit his mind with the plan to steal the Eastern Queen.

In that he saw a far more masterly will and daring personality than McCabe possessed, and very, very often on the trip had he wondered who the man was with whom McCabe had joined forces.

He only knew that he was a survivor from the Kara Maru, that he claimed the name of William Carr, that he also claimed to have been a seaman aboard the Kara Maru, and that deduction strongly associated him with the missing pearl.

To Blake's mind he loomed up as a very important factor in the case, and had he only known the identity of the so-called William Carr, it would have endorsed in a startling manner the mathematical results of his keen deduction.

But so far he did not dream that Rymer was mixed up in matters, but when he did discover that fact, it was to explain much that had puzzled him so far. Yet he did clothe the mysterious partner of Black McCabe with importance in the present state of things, and when he made his plans for discovering what he could ashore, he had the unknown man far more in mind than McCabe.

At his instigation the Fleur-de-Lys dropped anchor off shore, and lay, gently riding the swell, until nightfall. Just as they had anchored, a small steam launch had dashed past them, heading for the open sea, and little did Blake dream that she, too, was bound upon the business of the crimson pearl.

Not until dinner was over and the indigo of the tropical night had descended upon them, did Blake put into operation the plan upon which he had decided. First he went to his cabin, and from the trunk which had been transferred from the Eastern Queen, took a suit of rough garments.

Attiring himself in these, he next produced a heavy black beard and moustache, which he attached. A broad, soft hat completed the disguise, and when he had slipped his heavy automatic, fully loaded, into his pocket, he was ready for the purpose of the evening.

He made his way to the deck, and although he had resisted all Tinker's pleadings to accompany him, he did promise the lad that he should go in the boat as far as the shore, and remain in charge there until he returned from his mission.

Already a boat had been lowered, and was riding gently on the swell. Two of the sailors sat in it with muffled oars, and at the last moment Hendricks, the mate, joined the party. Then, when Blake and Tinker had dropped into the boat, they pushed off and headed for the beach.

Here and there could be seen the lights of the pearling vessels where they lay waiting for the coming of another day. Across the water came the noise of the workers as they opened the shell or stacked it for inspection. Blended with it was a medley of voices from every direction, some cursing and quarrelling, some singing, and some shouting to companions on another vessel.

Picking their way well out from the other boats, the sailors pulled past the long, treacherous reef which juts out just there and headed round the point. In ten minutes they were in the shadow of the shore, and in another two the nose of the boat grounded gently.

Then, with a last word, telling his companions he would be back as soon as possible, Blake drew his hat down over his eyes and made for the village. On reaching the collection of shacks which composed it, he made his way at once to the hotel, where a rough crowd was gathered in the bar.

As he pushed his way through and demanded a drink, a few curious glances were thrown in his direction, for he was at once spotted as a stranger. But after the first glance, the curious ones turned away.

Whoever the newcomer was, they decided he was an able customer, and from the cut of him he did not look like the type who would prove easy to pluck. On his part, Blake knew exactly what kind of a bunch he was up against, and acted accordingly.

When a huge specimen of humanity elbowed him unceremoniously, and growled at him, Blake quietly set his drink down, and dropping his hand to his hip, demanded to know if the muttered remark had been meant for him.

For a full minute his eyes held those of the giant; then the latter turned away. The steely menace in Blake's had conquered, and from that moment he was left in peaceful possession of his place.

Having created the necessary impression, and now satisfied that he could watch undisturbed, he ordered another drink, and, with it in his hand, ensconced himself in a corner. From where he sat he had a view of the whole place, and, though apparently absorbed in his own thoughts, his eyes were sweeping the faces of the occupants of the bar, searching, searching for that which he sought.

When the last countenance had been examined, he leaned back, disappointed. In all that medley of adventurers he did not see the face of Black McCabe. Even though the latter were disguised, Blake felt he would be certain to pierce it, and, knowing the nature of McCabe, he knew that were he in Thursday Island, he must sooner or later seek the circle which would appeal to him.

For fully half an hour he sat there, a silent spectator of what was understood by the men before him as amusement. Taken altogether, it was a bunch of about the choicest specimens to be found anywhere in the East, and it was a safe gamble that the majority of them would have responded to a name which was unlike the one which they had been born.

The crowd kept changing its personnel continually. Men kept passing out, while others came to take their places, and it was to the steady line of newcomers that Blake now turned his attention.

Another ten minutes went by before his patience was rewarded by anything of interest, but when it was Blake felt a sudden thrill shoot through him. At first he heard a voice in the passage outside the bar which he could have sworn, belonged to none other than Black McCabe.

Again he heard it, this time nearer, and, looking up as the swing door of the bar was pushed open, he expected to see McCabe come in.

First a hand came into view, then a shoulder, followed by a stalwart frame, and this it was which sent the thrill through Blake. It was not McCabe, but the long fingers which had curved round the edge of the door and the swing of the shoulders had struck a note in Blake which Black McCabe could never strike.

Cautiously Blake's eyes travelled upwards until they rested on the face of the man who had just come in, and as he mentally stripped the features of the bushy beard, he drew a long breath. No disguise could conceal that identity from Blake. Too many times he had studied it in the past, and as he realised it was Rymer indeed, his pulse quickened.

Just behind was Black McCabe, like a minor satellite about the greater planet, and when Blake saw that he was with Rymer, much that had been puzzling became suddenly clear. In a flash he realised that Rymer's was the superior brain which had planned and carried out the theft of the schooner.

Now he saw why his deductions had pointed to McCabe's mysterious partner as a man of greater calibre than he. Now it was indeed plain why it was possible that the sole survivor of the Kara Maru might also be the possessor of the crimson pearl.

The discovery of Rymer's connection with McCabe was, to Blake, like a sudden flood of light, upon a stage which had been obscured by shadow and peopled by spectres. To him was now visible the chief actor and prompter, and with the discovery came also a grim pleasure.

Rymer and McCabe paid no attention to Blake. To them he was but another of the men who thronged the place. They pushed their way to the bar, and, ordering, drank in silence.

Scarcely five minutes were they there before they turned to go out again, and as the swing door closed after them, Blake also rose. Lurching across the bar, he passed out, and kept along until he reached the street.

Just disappearing in the dusk were the two whom he was following. They were walking briskly along the main thoroughfare, apparently bound for the lower end of the sandy street where a bright light shone. Blake stepped off the verandah of the hotel, and started after them. The presence of other men in the street rendered his movements inconspicuous, and he was able to follow his quarry at fairly close quarters without risk of discovery.

He knew Thursday Island fairly well, and he knew Charlie Wong's gambling joint. Therefore it was not hard for him to guess where Rymer and McCabe were going, though in his own mind Blake wondered what strong motive was causing McCabe to risk a visit to such a public place as Charlie Wong's when he knew the risk even that lawless den had for him.

There was a matter of a thousand pounds reward for the capture of Black McCabe, and for that sum the men who frequented Charlie Wong's would betray their own brothers if there were no risk to themselves.

But whatever the reason, Blake was determined to discover it, if possible. Now that he had finally come up with his quarry, and discovered Rymer was mixed up in the affair, he had no intention of losing sight of either of them.

It may be asked why he did not expose McCabe at once, and have him arrested, but the answer to that is simple. In the first place, the representatives of law and order at Thursday Island are in the great minority, and were Blake to show his hand now, McCabe and Rymer might, if they succeeded in enlisting the temporary assistance of the tougher element, get clear.

Again, nothing was to be gained by a precipitate move, for, as yet, Blake had no idea what McCabe had done with the stuff he had stolen, and he would certainly not consider the capture of McCabe a success unless he recovered the stolen goods as well. Moreover, there was still the mystery of Rymer's connection with McCabe to settle, as well as to ferret out the whereabouts of the crimson pearl.

Therefore, Blake made caution his watchword, patience his banner, and strategy his plan of campaign, and so, grimly determined, he passed into Charlie Wong's gambling den hard on the heels of Rymer and McCabe.

The gaming-room was crowded. At no time could Charlie Wong complain of that department of his business, but on this particular night there was an even greater crowd than usual.

Two faro games were going full blast. Through the general murmur of the room came the monotonous call of the dealer, with the occasional monosyllabic utterances of the case-keeper.

Three poker tables were filled, and from the stacks of chips on the tables, it was evident that the stakes were high. Some Chinks and Japs were playing fan-tan in a corner, and even a roulette table was in operation. There was something for every gambler, and from the tense atmosphere of the room, it was evident that those who patronised the place did so with serious intent.

The bar was doing a rushing business. Two Kanaka boys were hurrying from table to table, taking orders and delivering drinks as fast as the two Celestials behind the bar could toss them up.

Over all hung a pall of smoke caused by the rising clouds from pipes, cigars, and cigarettes. It was altogether a complete gambling layout, patronised to the limit.

On first entering, Blake did not see the two men whom he had followed. At first he thought they must have passed through into another room, but, to assure himself, he sauntered along to a faro table, and under the pretence of watching the progress of the game, swept the room with his eyes. At last, through the smoke, he caught sight of them. They were both standing at the bar, and at the moment Rymer was talking to one of the barmen.

A moment later Blake saw the Chink leave the bar and come down the room. He kept on to a door at the far end, through which he disappeared. In less than five minutes he returned, and when he was once more behind the bar, Blake saw him bend over and whisper something to Rymer. The latter nodded, and, signing to McCabe, turned.

They came down the room as the Chinaman had done, and, in passing the faro table, Rymer's arm brushed that of Blake, so close were they. Blake kept his eyes on the table and did not move a muscle, though the actual contact had sent a thrill through him. Then the pair had passed, and disappeared the way the barman had gone before.

A good deal was now plain to Blake. In the first place, he had an explanation of why McCabe should risk coming to such a public place. It was not for the purpose of playing, but was to secure a private interview with someone.

He hadn't the slightest doubt but that it was Charlie Wong himself whom McCabe had come to see, for Blake had heard more than one rumour that the Celestial was a fence on a large scale.

In a flash, he read McCabe's purpose. It could be for no other reason than to get rid of the swag he had carried all the way from London, and, in the same moment, Blake realised that, if the booty once dropped into the secret channels controlled by Charlie Wong, it would never again see the light of day in its present form.

It would be melted down and sent into Oriental channels, which would utterly change its identity, and effectually baffle all efforts to trace the source from which it came. It was obvious to him that if he were to win out of the present situation, some radical move must be made.

Yet here on Thursday Island with him was the man he sought. Here, too, was Rymer, whom he thought was in possession of the crimson pearl. When he remembered the dead Chinaman he had seen in Cabin 20 of the sunken Kara Maru, Blake saw more than a coincidence in Rymer's visit to Charlie Wong.

That the junk containing San was but an echo of the fruitless journey of the dead Chinaman on the Kara Maru, seemed a certainty. That Charlie Wong was part and parcel of San's system also seemed probable. Big as he was, Charlie Wong was an insignificant factor compared with San.

But was Rymer friend or foe of the Celestial element? Was his seeking out of Wong but a preliminary to receiving a share for the pearl, or was he playing a lone hand, and had he sought Charlie Wong in order to negotiate for the sale of the pearl, ignorant that San, of all people, was the head and front of the Chinese crowd?

Taken altogether, it was a profound problem, a puzzling maze, a bewildering array of wheels within wheels. It was no cinch to jump into that yellow tangle and win a double —the pearl and Black McCabe. But its very difficulties but served to rouse in Blake all the obstinate determination the man possessed, and though he was playing for big stakes on slim chances, he was as cool as the heaviest plunger in a falling market.

What was going on behind that door by way of which Rymer and McCabe had gone he had no idea. For him to follow was out of question. The place was too well guarded for him to slip through secretly, and yet he had a strong idea that if he only knew what was being said back there he would be a long way ahead.

All the time these thoughts were racing through his mind, Blake was leaning over the faro table. Once or twice he had staked, and, winning, had mechanically gathered up the chips.

Fully an hour passed, and still Rymer and McCabe did not reappear. He was just wondering if they had gone out by some back exit, when the door at the end of the room opened, and they entered.

A swift glance told Blake that their interview had been of a pleasing description, for in Black McCabe's eyes lurked a gleam of satisfaction.

They approached the bar once more, and after drinking, turned to survey the room. Blake saw McCabe turn and say something to Rymer. The latter nodded, tossed off his drink, and led the way down the room straight to the faro layout where Blake was standing.

They both bought chips, and began staking moderately. Rymer took his luck indifferently, but McCabe lost the caution he had practised in the lure of the game, and more than once Blake heard Rymer speak sharply to him.

Another quarter of an hour passed, then the door at the upper end of the room opened, and a Chinaman entered. Through the cloud of smoke Blake did not recognise him, but as he walked slowly down between the tables he felt a sharp stab of wonder.

At first he could hardly believe his eyes. They told him it was San —San the cunning, whom he had seen on the junk away back in Rubilinga. But if it were, he could not fathom how the Celestial could now be in Thursday Island.

In the swiftly steaming Fleur-de-Lys he himself had only arrived that day, and it seemed utterly impossible that the clumsy junk could have made the trip so quickly. Yet, as the newcomer drew still nearer, Blake saw that it was San, and no other.

It was but natural that he should be puzzled over the matter, for he did not know that San had followed the yacht from Rubilinga, and that a fair wind had sent the junk lumbering along at a good clip.

Nor did he know of the speedy steam launch which had raced away from Thursday Island early that afternoon, in order to find San.

Far out in the Straits it had met the junk, and after reading Charlie Wong's letter. San had returned in the launch. The junk was not yet in sight of the island, nor would she make it until the following morning.

San regarded the gamblers with superb indifference, and kept on until he reached the door at the lower end of the room. At the very moment when his hand was going out towards the handle, the door opened, and on the threshold appeared Charlie Wong. Blake saw him give a surprised look at San, then his eyes conveyed a message of some kind, and he at once turned back, followed by San.

As the two disappeared, Blake took a handful of chips and bent far over the table on the pretext of placing them between the six and seven. He "buttoned" them to "lose," and deliberately fumbled the "button" while he bent still more in order to hear a remark Rymer was making to McCabe. He caught the words "wait a while," then he was compelled to straighten up, yet not before he had received his cue.

From that on he played steadily until the door at the lower end of the room again opened, and Charlie Wong appeared. His gaze swept over the place until he located Rymer and McCabe. Then he sauntered across until he was close to the table.

Just as he reached it, Blake once more bent over to place a bet, and as Wong passed Rymer, Blake heard him murmur in Chinese: "Come to-morrow night at ten." He saw Rymer nod without shifting his gaze from the table, then Charlie Wong had passed on, and Blake straightened up.

Hard on this Rymer and Black McCabe cashed in, and moved away. They stopped for a few minutes at the bar, then continued on to the door and passed out.

Ten minutes later Blake also departed, but he made no attempt to follow the other two. He made straight for the beach with but one phrase drumming in his mind, and that phrase was the one Charlie Wong had uttered to Rymer.

BLAKE was uncommunicative on his way back to the yacht, and when he arrived there, instead of joining Yvonne and the Lamports aft, he went straight to his cabin. Once there he closed the door and bolted it.

His first move was to remove his disguise and to get into thin clothes. Then he turned out the light, and, casting himself down, gave his whole mind to the problem in hand.

He laid out all the facts he had gathered, and when he had deduced what he could from the evidence in hand he had built up a fairly complete framework which he felt would support the conclusions arrived at.

First and foremost, he had discovered his deductions made back at Rubilinga to be correct. The man who had accompanied McCabe seemed to be the most likely possessor of the crimson pearl.

Secondly, he had discovered the identity of that man.

Thirdly, he had at last succeeded in running McCabe to earth. As he had prophesied, the path leading to McCabe and that leading to the possessor of the pearl had been one and the same.

Furthermore, the puzzling connection with the affair of San and Charlie Wong seemed a good deal clearer. That murmured remark of Charlie Wong's as he passed the faro table showed that the words he uttered to Rymer indicated that a decision had been arrived at after he had talked with San.

Therefore, it was evident that whatever business Rymer had with him had of necessity been delayed until San put in an appearance. What was the most likely reason for such a thing?

Blake argued that, supposing Rymer possessed the pearl, and also supposing he desired to dispose of it to the Celestials, he would have to seek those who could swing a big sum.

In Thursday Island no more likely man could be found than Charlie Wong, but even supposing he could raise the necessary sum, Blake knew there might be a dozen different reasons why he could not act without San's sanction. The ramifications of Oriental purposes are at all times of a far-reaching nature.

At any rate, it looked like a certainty that Rymer and McCabe were to be at Charlie Wong's the next night at ten o'clock, and if Blake were ever to win on the present deal, he would have to turn not one trick but several tricks in his favour before the purposes of the enemy had been carried into effect.

The sum total of his ruminations was the evolving of a plan which seemed the only one to fit the case of such urgency, though it was fraught with no little danger and threatened to produce a denouement which might lead to a battle royal.

With this decision Blake turned in and calmly dropped off to sleep. Early the next morning he was brought back to present day affairs by a loud knocking at his door.

"Hallo! What is it?" he called drowsily.

"It is I, guv'nor," came in Tinker's voice. "What do you think has happened?"

"Having just awakened, I can't say," answered Blake drily. "What is it?"

"The Eastern Queen has just arrived, guv'nor, and Captain Weeks is aboard the yacht. He says they passed a junk just outside which was beating in, and he thinks it is the same one which was off Rubilinga."

"You can go up on deck and tell Captain Weeks that his eyes have not deceived him, my lad. It is the same junk all right. By the way, Tinker, do you remember the steam launch which left here yesterday when we cast anchor?"

"Yes, sir."

"Have a look round and see if you can sight her anywhere. I am curious to know if she has returned."

"Why, guv'nor, she —or one just like her —came in last night when we were waiting on the beach for you."

"Ah!"

For a moment after he uttered the monosyllable Blake was silent, then he called:

"All right, my lad. I will be on deck shortly. Detain Captain Weeks. I wish to speak with him."

Tinker departed on his errand, and Blake rose at once. While he dressed he went over in his mind the result of his ponderings the previous night, and when, in the morning light, he still considered the decision he had made the best one, he felt that he was right.

What Tinker had told him about the launch made still another point clear. He saw now how it was possible for San to have arrived as mysteriously sudden as he had, and it but went to strengthen his opinion that the final move in the game would be played in Charlie Wong's gambling joint that night.

When he had finished dressing he made his way to the deck, where he found Captain and Mrs. Lamport, Yvonne, and Captain Weeks.

After greeting them he cast his eyes about at the panorama which lay spread before him, then he turned to them.

"I must apologise for not appearing last night when I returned," he said, smiling down into Yvonne's eyes. "But the truth is I made one or two discoveries of an important nature, and went straight to my cabin to think them over."

"Then you found out something?" she asked.

He nodded.

"Yes —a great deal, in a way. But gather closer everyone, and I will tell you.

"In the first place, the man I am after is here. I saw him — almost touched him last night. Furthermore, the man who joined him and helped to steal your schooner, Captain Weeks, is here, too.

"When I tell you whom it is, I can guarantee a surprise for you —at least for Yvonne, Captain Vaughan, and Tinker. It is Dr. Huxton Rymer."

"Rymer!" exclaimed Yvonne. "Then —why, then, according to your idea, Mr. Blake, it is Rymer who possesses Captain Lamport's pearl."

"Exactly. Moreover, I think he is already negotiating with a Celestial here for the sale of it, and that Celestial's principal is, in my opinion, none other than San. But I will tell you exactly what occurred last night."

Briefly he related what he had seen, from the moment he landed until he returned to the yacht. Then he took them with him along the paths of thought he had followed, showing them how and why he had arrived at the conclusion he had. It took some time, but the rapt silence of his hearers showed how absorbed they were in what he had to say. When he had finished Yvonne spoke.

"You say you have arrived at a decision?"

Blake nodded.

"Yes, as I told you, I think things will come a crisis to-night. That means, if we are to act at all we must act then.

"I have gone over every point, and in forming the plan I propose presenting I have considered every aspect of the case. Now this is what I propose:

"This afternoon I shall go ashore and procure the co-operation of the police official stationed here. To-night I shall go ashore again, and my idea is to have a large force accompany me. With Captain Vaughan, Captain Weeks, Hendricks, Tinker, and a fair number of the sailors, we should have a party equal to any emergency which may crop up.

"I tell you frankly I anticipate trouble, and for it we must go prepared. Neither Rymer nor McCabe are going to give in without a struggle. Rymer will realise what he stands to lose, and McCabe will know that it is his last stand. Therefore, they will both resist to their utmost.

"We know San of old. We know to what lengths he is prepared to go, and if they succeed in gaining the temporary aid of the crowd which haunts Charlie Wong's, there will be trouble in earnest.

"However, I intend going. Those who come must all volunteer, but, from what I know of the sailors, I imagine the only difficulty will be to persuade them that some must remain here.

"I do not think it is wise for Captain Lamport to go. It is better for him to stay here and protect the ladies in case any side move is made. Now, then, what do you all think of my proposal?"

A chorus of eager assent answered, and with a smile Blake said:

"Very well, then, it is settled. After breakfast we will call the men together and lay the matter before them."

"I'd like to say one thing," put in Captain Weeks grimly.

"What is it, captain?"

"It is this. I want room kept in the party for my own two men. They both have scores to settle with those pirates, and they deserve the chance."

"In view of the stealing of the schooner, I think that is only fair," responded Blake. "Places will be kept for both of them, captain."

They all trooped down to breakfast in a state of subdued excitement. One and all felt that before they were gathered about the table for their next breakfast much indeed might happen. And much was to happen.

After breakfast they returned to the deck, where Captain Vaughan had the sailors lined up. In a few brief words Blake told them that an expedition ashore was to be undertaken that night, that there might be serious trouble, and were any of them prepared to volunteer for duty?

A delighted grin appeared on the countenance of every one of Yvonne's devoted sea-dogs, and every hand shot up. Just as Blake had anticipated, the trouble was to be to decide which to take and which to leave behind. It was finally settled by casting lots, and that end of the matter settled, Blake made preparations to go ashore.

It took him a considerable portion of the afternoon to arrange with the representatives of law and order in Thursday Island that he should have a comparatively free hand that night. Only the exceptional nature of Blake's credentials gained him his point without the necessity for divulging all his reasons. But after a strenuous two hours he returned to the beach triumphant.

During the time he had been ashore he had sedulously avoided the neighbourhood of Charlie Wong's place and the hotel. He had no fancy for being recognised, realising that such a thing would endanger his well-laid plans for that night.

He returned to the yacht in a state of satisfaction. As far as he could, he had prepared for every eventuality, and now nothing remained to be done but to wait for nightfall. All hands on board spent the afternoon in a quiet manner, lounging about, and discussing the outlook for the night.

Forward, the men were busy cleaning revolvers and knives, and from time to time a low laugh floated aft as some one of them made a humorous remark about the fray they devoutly hoped was coming.

Dinner was served early, and after coffee on deck Blake went below. He donned the same outfit he had worn the previous night, but on this occasion slipped an extra revolver into his pocket. Then he returned to the deck, where the others awaited him.

Ten of the crew had been picked to go, leaving four on the yacht. With Blake, Captain Weeks, Captain Vaughan, Hendricks, Tinker, and the two men from the Eastern Queen, it made a party of seventeen in all —seventeen hardened and experienced veterans who would offer a tough problem to the toughest element.

As he looked them over where they stood by the rail, a glow of satisfaction swept over Blake. It was good to have a force like that behind him when carrying the fight into a place like that of Charlie Wong's. All were dressed in dark garments —Blake and his companions in rough tweeds, and the sailors in their dark serge uniforms.

The long boat had already been lowered, and rocked gently alongside waiting for them to descend. Before giving the word, Blake stood before them and addressed them in low tones:

"You all know the rendezvous," he said quietly, "On reaching the beach you will separate. In parties of two or three you will make your way into the town and lounge about the street. Work your way along until you come to the gambling place. Then get together.

"You will not enter until you get the signal. It will be a shot, and if you hear it lose no time. Rush the door and get through into the gambling room at once. As you enter you will see a door at the opposite side. Make for it. Most of the trouble will probably take place beyond it.

"It will be well for three or four to remain outside the place. I will leave it to Captain Vaughan to pick the men necessary for that.

"A last word. I hope to accomplish my purpose without trouble, but if you do get the signal come on the run. That is all. Now into the boat."

Man after man tumbled over the side, and slid down to the boat below. As each one went, Yvonne uttered a soft word of encouragement, reserving a lingering pressure of the hand for Blake, the last to go. Then the boat was let go, and with muffled oars, they pulled softly for the shore.

On reaching the beach, they drew the boat up in a shadowy spot, and immediately separated. There was little danger that any suspicion would be aroused by the presence of the sailors, for it was a natural thing that they should have shore leave.

Captain Weeks and his two men went off together, Hendricks, the mate, went with some of the sailors, Tinker moved off with Captain Vaughan, and when they had all disappeared, Blake started off alone.

He sauntered up the main street in an aimless manner. Glancing at his watch, he saw that it was exactly a quarter to ten. The street held a fair number of pedestrians for it was a hot night, and as he passed the opened doors of several bars, Blake could see they were doing a rushing business.

Here and there he caught sight of the blue uniform of Yvonne's sailors as they stood about in the saloons, and once in the distance, he saw Tinker and Captain Vaughan sauntering along. Then he came to Charlie Wong's place, and pushing open the outer door strode in.

As he expected, the place was already full. Even more men were gathered about than on the previous night. They were a tough looking crew, and as he sized them up, Blake realised they would form a nasty obstacle to the success of his plans if trouble developed, and they swung to the side of Charlie Wong.

He looked quite as tough as any of them with his bushy beard and flannel shirt thrown open at the neck. For his part, he wore a coat, but many of those present did not, and hanging to the hips of most of them were heavy revolvers —a frank acknowledgment that they went heeled, prepared for trouble.

Blake sauntered across to the bar, and, ordering a drink, surveyed the room, while he sipped it. He was waiting for Rymer and McCabe to put in appearance, and knew they were not likely to be late. Nor were they.

He had been standing at the bar for less than ten minutes, when the door opened, and in they came. A sharp thrill went through Blake as he saw McCabe was carrying a bulky package, and from the manner in which he held it it was easy to see that it was heavy.

Rymer led the way straight towards the door at the far end of the gambling room. Blake saw him rap on it sharply, saw it open almost at once, saw a yellow-faced Celestial interrogate them, then they passed through, and the door closed after them.

Another ten minutes went by before Blake moved. Then straightening up, he made his way slowly between the tables. He kept on until he reached the door through which the other two had gone, and with a strange, steely glint in his eye, raised his hand, and knocked twice.

A shuffling noise came from the other side, and a moment later the door swung back. He saw before him the same Celestial who had opened to Rymer and McCabe, and before he had time to speak, Blake pushed inside.

"What you want?" demanded the other sharply in broken English.

Blake bent low, and gazed straight into the other's eyes.

"Close the door," he said in Chinese. "I come to see his Excellency. It is of the utmost urgency. Lead me to him."

For a moment the man wavered. He had received orders to admit the other two, but nothing had been said about the man who stood before him. It seemed irregular, yet the assurance of the big bearded man seemed to arise from a certainty that he would be welcomed. Blake bent closer.

"Did you hear me?" he snapped. "Do you wish to have the wrath of his Excellency descend upon you?"

That remark was just the one needed to carry his bluff. The Chink turned without a word and closed the door, then with a grunt, he led the way along the passage.

And as he followed after Blake realised that the die was cast. There was no going back now even had he wished to, which he did not. It was a case of his brains and strategy against those of a choice quartette of scoundrels, and though the odds were heavy against him, Blake tingled with anticipation as he drew momentarily nearer to his goal.

At last his guide stopped before a door, and knocked. A guttural voice replied, and the Chinaman lifted his arm to open the door. But Blake was before him. Thrusting him aside, he pushed open the door.

At first he seemed to have stepped into a room of darkness, but in a moment he saw that this impression was due to the curtains which hung down on the inside. Drawing them aside, he peered forth, and a barely perceptible click of his teeth sounded as he regarded the scene before him.

It was the inner room which was used for Charlie Wong's most private transactions. Nor did its bizarre appearance lose anything in the strange company which was gathered about the big teakwood desk at the far end.

In the massive chair usually occupied by Charlie Wong sat San. Blake recognised him at once. Not for a long time had he been so close to him, and the glimpse he had had of him through the glasses at Rubilinga had been the first for many months.

But he had not altered a whit since the adventurous days when he had been the right hand man of Prince Wu Ling. Perhaps he was a trifle more corpulent, but that was hard to tell owing to the loose flowing tunic he wore.

Blake noted in one swift glance that a greater dignity sat upon him, as though he had inherited a portion of the inimitable aloofness which had been an inherent part of Wu Ling. He noted also, and with no little surprise, that San affected the saffron colour which had been the sole privilege of Wu Ling.

He wondered if the Brotherhood of the Yellow Beetle had been reorganised under San, and if the latter were endeavouring to carry on the gigantic plan which had been the life aim of the prince.

His gaze shifted to Charlie Wong who sat at San's right hand, then in a swift glance he took in Rymer and McCabe. Every one of them was gazing back at him —the two white men with a suspicious frown, the two Celestials with imperturbable expression.

Then his eyes went back to San, and with his right hand hanging close to his hip he moved forward. Half way he got before a word was spoken. Then San opened his lips, and uttered a sharp exclamation.

"Halt!" he said.

Not prepared yet to show his hand, Blake did so.

"Who are you? How did you get in here? And what do you want?" he asked in English.

Blake did not answer at once. His eyes had caught sight of a great heap of gold and notes on the desk, and instinctively he knew it was McCabe's swag. A moment only, then he met San's eyes with a level glance.

"Who am I, how did I get in here, and what do I want?" he repeated softly. "I will tell you, your Excellency —San."

Dead silence followed his use of the Celestial's name. Rymer and McCabe dropped their hands to their hips with an uncertain gesture, but San waved them to be still.

"Well," he said evenly.

"Who I am I will tell you presently," went on Blake. "How I got in is easily answered. I walked in. And what I want is also easily answered. I want three things, and I have come to get them."

"What are they?"

Blake stood easily, hands resting negligently on his hips. He looked utterly relaxed, and apparently at the mercy of any of them who chose to draw and fire. But he was far from unprepared.

Only those who had seen Blake in action knew with what incredible swiftness he could draw a gun. One motion of the wrist, a backward jerk, a lightning-like crook of the finger and so quickly that the eye could not follow his gun was out.

And that is exactly what he did now. He saw Rymer and McCabe still feeling at their guns, and though they had less to do, their hands were still resting on the butts when Blake drew and covered them.

"All hands on the desk," he drawled.

They obeyed without hesitation. This stranger who had forced his way in, had business in his eye. They were content to submit for the moment, and wait for a chance to turn the tables. With a single sweep, Blake removed his beard, and smiled at the stupefied McCabe.

"Rather a surprise, McCabe," he said in the same drawling tones. "I suppose you thought my bones were already beneath the soil back in Rubilinga. No thanks to you that they are not."

Then he turned to San whom he saw had recognised him.

"I am sorry to break in upon such a profitable moment, San," he said mockingly. "However, it was necessary. Now I will answer your other two questions— or rather one. It is needless to proclaim my identity. As to what I want I will tell you.

"Firstly I want Black McCabe, secondly I want that bunch of swag on the table, and thirdly I want the crimson pearl. Do I get them?"

With a smothered exclamation, Rymer started up.

"How in —" he began.

"How did I know you had the crimson pearl?" drawled Blake. "Is that what you would ask? Very, simple, my dear Rymer. I knew it in the same way I knew it was you, and not McCabe, who planned the piracy of the Eastern Queen.

"I must congratulate you, Rymer, or shall I say William Carr, on your marvellous escape from the Kara Maru. It was a wonderful piece of luck. Perhaps the details would interest you, San, or do you already know them? When you went down to the Kara Maru I presume you saw the dead man. Who killed Ferguson, Rymer? Was it you or the dead Celestial?"

"By heavens! You —devil," snarled Rymer.

"What, are you surprised at my knowledge?" mocked Blake. "Did you think you had got clear without leaving a trail? My dear Rymer you were very careless. But come, I can see San would like to know how his fellow countryman on the Kara Maru met his death."

"I tell you I did not kill him," blurted Rymer with an uneasy glance at San.

"Ah!" said Blake, and in the next moment, Rymer saw what a slip he had made.

Again Blake turned to San.

"Well, San," he said, dropping his mocking tone. "How about it? Do I get what I want? Or have I got to take it?"

San leaned forward on the desk and smiled. But what a smile it was. All the menace of the East seemed contained in it.

"No!" he whispered sibilantly.

"Then I must take them?" inquired Blake in the same tone that he might have asked for the salt.

"If you can," answered San smiling again.

With a single motion, Blake raised his revolver, and sent a shot crashing into the ceiling. Like a flash the four men at the desk leaped to their feet.

"What does that mean?" asked San sharply.

"Do I get what I want?" snapped Blake, ignoring the question.

"No!"

"Then I will tell you what that shot means. Rymer! Keep your hand away from your gun! McCabe, if you move an inch I will put a bullet through your black heart. Now then, San, that shot was a signal. I have enough men outside to back up my demands. For the third and last time do I get what I want?"

San did not reply. His eyes were fixed on something just over Blake's shoulder, and so busy was the latter watching that none of them drew on him that at first he did not see the direction of San's gaze.

But when the Celestial did not reply, Blake glanced at him. For a moment he stood rigid. In the distance he could hear the sound of many crashes, and the loud voices of angered men.

Then suddenly, a nearer sound reached his ears, and with the quickness of a panther he sprang to one side. At the same instant something flashed down past his shoulder, slitting his sleeve to the wrist and, as he caught the flash of light on a flying blade, an arm followed it, and a Celestial crashed to the floor, over-balanced by the force of the blow which had missed.

Without the slightest hesitation, Blake sent a shot crashing into the would-be assassin's shoulder, then he swung back to the quartette at the desk. But though he had escaped the fate intended for him, the moment necessary for him to turn had given the others the chance they needed.

Both Rymer and McCabe had drawn and, quick though he was to fire, their shots rang out simultaneously with Blake's. Blake felt a shock against his left arm, then a burning pain; but in the same moment he saw McCabe stagger back.

Then came a terrific crash behind him, followed by a pandemonium of shrieks and shots, curses and yells, and in the same moment San leaped for a button, sending the room into darkness.

A red flame split the darkness as Rymer fired again, and Blake returned the compliment before the echo had died away, aiming for the spot where he had seen the flash. Then he leaped aside just as another flash and roar came.

Hard on this the sounds of conflict drew nearer, and the door crashed in.

"Guv'nor! Guv'nor!" he heard in Tinker's shrill accents.

"Right here, my lad!" he shouted, then dodged, as Rymer again fired.

A rush of feet sounded behind him, as Tinker and several others rushed in. Blake began firing in the direction of the desk, but suddenly he noticed that no shots were returned.

It flashed upon him that Rymer had been doing all the firing anyway, and from the very first San, and Charlie Wong had been strangely silent. McCabe he knew had been struck by his first shot.

Shouting to Tinker and the others to hold their fire, he dashed forward until he stumbled against the desk. Feeling his way around it, he searched for the wall and found it. Then, judging as well as he could where San had stood when he had switched out the lights, he ran his hand up and down.

A grunt of satisfaction escaped him as his fingers encountered the switch. He turned it quickly, and as the room was once more flooded with light he swung sharply, on guard against attack.

He saw Tinker, Captain Vaughan and three of the sailors standing with levelled revolvers blinking at the light. He saw the Celestial who had tried to murder him lying unconscious on the floor. But of San, Charlie Wong, Rymer or McCabe, there was not the faintest sign.

It was exactly as if they had been swallowed up by the floor. And to prove that their disappearance had not been unduly hasty, all the swag which had been on the desk was gone too.

But that did not strike Blake as very surprising. He knew he was in a Chinese den, and knew it was a safe bet that the place was honeycombed with secret passages. He knew also that they might search for an hour before finding one. Turning sharply to Captain Vaughan he cried:

"Did you leave some men outside, captain?"

"Yes —five altogether. But unless I am mistaken, we will need them inside. Our men are having it tough in the gaming room."

"Then come on," rapped Blake. "Our quarry may make for there."

He dashed for the door as he spoke, and went racing down the passage, followed by the others. As he burst into the gambling room, he saw a sight which would live in his memory for ever.

From end to end the room was filled by a swaying mass of struggling men —some standing off shooting indiscriminately, some firing from shelter, some clubbing and knifing, but most fighting at close quarters.

Almost every table had been upset and smashed; chairs were like matchwood, bottles, cards, glasses and chips had been crunched and scattered underfoot. Here and there, in the midst of the wreckage, lay men who had gone down in the melee.

From every side came the cursing grunts of strong men battling, and over all hung the pungent odorous smoke —that of powder, mixed with that of tobacco. It was a wild scene.

In a single glance Blake saw that his men were fearfully outnumbered, for the habitues of the place had thrown in their lot with Charlie Wong's men. Looking further, he saw Rymer swaying in the midst of a struggling mass, like a sturdy oak bending beneath the blast.

Sheltered behind a table was Black McCabe, shooting with his one good hand. San was over behind the bar with two heavy automatics, shooting slowly and precisely. On the bar itself stood Charlie Wong, shrieking like a maniac, and urging his adherents on to greater efforts.

Captain Weeks and his two men were in a melee with half a dozen gamblers; Hendricks and the sailors were fighting like madmen. A moment only it took to size up the situation, then, with a hoarse cry, Blake dashed into the fray, followed by Captain Vaughan, Tinker and the others.

Blake headed straight for the struggling mass of which Rymer was the centre. A ring of gamblers surrounded him, striking out with him. Attacking were two of the sailors and Hendricks. The latter turned as Blake dashed in, but said nothing, and a moment later Blake was into it, fighting tooth and nail to reach Rymer.

Out of the corner of his eye he caught a glimpse of Tinker making for Black McCabe, and saw Captain Vaughan opening fire on Charlie Wong. Then, for some time, he lost all record of what was going on elsewhere. He only knew that a terrific rage possessed him, and that a boiling impatience filled him to reach Rymer.

Shoulder to shoulder with Hendricks he fought, clubbing and striking fiercely. Bearded face after bearded face came up before him, only to go down. Someone had reached his left shoulder with a knife, for though he did not feel the pain, he was conscious of a hot drip down his arm. Rymer was fighting magnificently and, be it said, made no attempt to escape meeting Blake.

The whole body of men shifted and swayed about, fighting, cursing, sweating, until, at last, as he sent the butt of his revolver crashing into a bearded face, Blake found himself face to face with Rymer.

Instinctively, each man braced himself for the shock, then they were into it. There was no time for feinting, there was no room for strategy. They were too close to use their revolvers. It was a case of brute strength, and in that they were evenly matched.

All about them the struggling mass reeled and tossed like a whirlpool; yet by common consent, the two were left to fight it out alone. Straight for Rymer's throat went Blake, and straight for his came Rymer, Blake gripped first and ducked.

He felt Rymer's hands curl in beneath his chin, but he stiffened the muscles of his neck and surged forward, feeling for a leg lock. At that moment the crowd swayed against them, and in the momentary heave, he gained his point, putting Rymer on the defensive.

Abandoning his attempt to reach Blake's throat, Rymer jabbed in an uppercut which, had it reached its intended destination on the point of Blake's chin, would have settled him then and there. But he caught the hook on his shoulder, and lurching still more met another.

Changing his tactics, Rymer worked his arms down, and began to send in a hail of body blows. Blake grunted, but did not yield, and then another lurch of the crowd jerked his hands from Rymer's throat. They grappled and hung on, waiting.

Rymer moved first. With a slow, twisting caution he worked his arm down, but just as he was drawing it back, Blake broke away, and shot up a jab that sent Rymer's head back and caused him to rock on his heels. He came back with a half-arm bore to the body, and followed with right and left to the head, but Blake caught the first on his arm, and the other two he sidestepped.

They were a little apart now, panting and glaring at each other with their full intent in their eyes. Blake feinted for the body, then bent and bored in with his right.

Again they clinched, Rymer holding on and boring his thumbs into the muscles of Blake's arms. But Blake worked his right down and, holding with his left, pushed back.

One —two —three! He whipped his arm up thrice in quick succession, catching Rymer on the jaw. Again they broke, but this time Blake followed up. He sent over a hard left to the jaw, then followed by a right hook and, dashing in, worked a hail of body blows that had Rymer dazed.

Still the latter came back with a straight left which broke through Blake's guard, and sent him rocking. He followed it up but, feinting with his left, Blake sidestepped and sent in a stinging right. It caught Rymer square on the point of the jaw, he reeled, came again, met a smashing left and dropped.

Panting, Blake dropped beside him, and tore open the neck of his shirt. Around Rymer's neck was a cord, and following it Blake felt a small leather bag. Jerking it out he tore it from the string, and ran his fingers over it.

"Got it! Got it!" he jerked out, for the moment blind and deaf to the turmoil about him.

He had no time to verify his supposition but, stuffing into his pocket the little bag which he hoped contained the crimson pearl, he straightened up to see Charlie Wong racing for him with a great knife in his hand.

Once more a great rage surged over Blake and he drew back. On came the Celestial, and from the blood lust in his eyes Blake knew Wong had seen him take the bag from Rymer's neck.

In a moment Wong came up and, poising his knife, sent it hurtling for Blake's heart. Just as it left the Chinaman's hand Blake dropped flat. It whistled wickedly over his head and Wong followed it.

But Blake came up again as though his limbs were steel springs and, clubbing his revolver, brought it down with all his strength between Charlie Wong's eyes. The Chink dropped as though he had been poleaxed, and Blake staggered clear.

For the first moment since he had dashed into the fray, he had an opportunity to see how things were going. A single glance told him that the hard fighting sailors were winning, though not without severe punishment.

Several of them were down, and many of those who were still in the fray, showed the mark of battle. Captain Vaughan and Hendricks were both down, and neither Captain Weeks nor Tinker were to be seen.

A hurried look round showed Blake that McCabe was missing also. Then he looked towards the bar. As he did so, he saw San just coming over it, and he dashed forward.

But San was not coming out to take a hand. He had done much damage with his shooting, but he was no fool, and when both Rymer and Charlie Wong had gone down, he saw how the fight must end.

It was easy to discern too that the gamblers were growing sick of the slaughter. They hadn't an idea what they were fighting about, but had accepted Charlie Wong's statement that it was a police raid.

San held up his hand as Blake dashed up, and the latter stopped.

"Well," he jerked, "what is it, San?"

"I surrender —on terms."

"What are they?"

"That you leave the place now."

"I will leave when I get what I want."

"You mean?"

"Only two things now," answered Blake grimly. "Black McCabe and his swag."

A whistling sound escaped the Celestial.

"Then Charlie Wong was right. You have the pearl?"

Blake nodded.

"Yes, and I intend handing it over to the proper quarter. But come, San, if you surrender, call off your men."

"I will, but first let me tell you something, Sexton Blake. You have done a foolish thing to mix up in this thing. When you did for the prince, I swore to get you, and now I tell you that I will.

"For the present you win; but I will catch you one day, and then— Moreover, the fight for that pearl is not yet over. It may go to the West; but it came from the East, and to the East it will return. Do we understand each other?"

"Perfectly, San," drawled Blake. "Now call off your men."

The Celestial turned, and sent up three sharp, shrill cries. At the first one the combatants paused, at the second they turned, and at the third they backed away.

In the momentary lull San addressed his side, telling them the dispute had been settled.

Even before he finished the sailors sent up a hoarse cheer, then hurried towards the prostrate Captain Vaughan and Hendricks.

Blake turned to San and rapped out just one word.

"McCabe!"

San pointed to the door at the far end.

"I saw him go that way. The lad was after him. Come, I will show you."

"All right, lead on; but if you try any tricks, San, I will drop you."

The Chinaman shrugged.

"When was San a fool?" he asked. "I know when to strike, I know when to hold my hand, and I know how to wait."

Blake followed him along the wrecked room and through the doorway, where the shattered door now hung uselessly. They kept on up the passage until they reached Wong's private room at the end.

San went in first, and, as he followed after, Blake saw that they had come to the right place. Beside the teakwood desk lay Tinker, limp and unconscious, but he was lying across the inert form of Black McCabe. And just beyond them, where McCabe had jerked it from beneath the desk, was the loot.

San made a gesture of disgust.

"You are welcome to him," he grunted. "When he saw the fight going against us he tried to save his own skin."

"And had he not stopped for the loot he might have succeeded," muttered Blake, as he dropped on his knees beside Tinker.

It was easy to see how the lad had brought down his man before going under himself. On his own forehead was a great bruise where the butt of McCabe's gun had caught him; but the crook's face was one terrible bruise, and still resting on it was Tinker's revolver.

Blake turned the lad gently, and, taking out his flask, poured some raw spirit between his lips.

Tinker's eyes opened, and he stared about vaguely, then they closed again.

A second dose of the spirits, however, revived him, and, as intelligence crept back into his eyes, he sat up.

"Scott! Guv'nor, my head!" he whispered. "How about McCabe? Did he get away?"

Blake smiled and pointed.

"There he is, my lad. Thanks to you he did not get away. But how do you feel?"

Tinker rubbed his head slowly.

"A bit sore and shaky, guv'nor, but I guess I'm still in the ring. How is the fight going?"

"It is all over, my lad. We won."

And, dazed though he was, Tinker gave vent to a feeble hurrah, which sounded more like the croak of a frog than anything else.

Blake smiled again, and lifted him to his feet. After that he bent and, using a strip of silk torn from the hangings of the room, bound the unconscious McCabe.

"A long chase, and he wasn't worth it," he muttered as he rose, and in that phrase he summed up the record of all his recent adventures.

San seated himself at the desk as Blake turned to go.

"How about Rymer?" he asked.

Blake shrugged.

"I have no authority to take him, and besides, I don't know that I wish to —this time."

He beckoned to Tinker then, and together they made their way to the door.

On arriving at the gambling room they found that Captain Vaughan and Hendricks were on their feet again.

Though severely battered, they were not seriously injured, and were highly pleased when Blake reported the complete success of the raid.

Captain Weeks appeared just then, and he was the only dissatisfied one in the crowd.

When McCabe had dashed out of the gaming-room with Tinker at his heels Captain Weeks had followed, still determined to be avenged upon the men who had stolen the Eastern Queen. He had taken a wrong turning, however, and ever since had been trying to find his way back.

One of the sailors had a very severe knife-wound in the shoulder, and another had a shattered arm where a bullet had caught him; but, with these two exceptions, the wounds were not serious.

Blake sent two of the sailors back for McCabe, while the rest of them bound up each other's wounds.

Over by the bar the gamblers and Chinks were taking count of their own casualties, and, although they glared menacingly at the victors, they did not offer to attack again.

Charlie Wong had come to, and now, staggering across the floor, he stood in front of Blake.

"Hang you!" he said, in a whisper. "I will get you yet."

"San has already informed me to that effect, Charlie," drawled Blake coolly. "Rest assured I shall be ready for you. When Rymer comes to give him my regards, and tell him the crimson pearl is now in safe hands."

With that Blake smiled mockingly, and the helpless Celestial turned away, fuming.

When the two sailors returned, carrying McCabe, Blake got his party together and started for the beach. Outside, those who had been on watch took a hand at carrying the wounded, and in this fashion the little party of bruised and battered victors made their way to the boat.

They rowed over to the yacht in silence, and there willing hands hoisted them aboard.

The last to go up was Blake, and when he swung over the side he carried in his arms Black McCabe's London loot.

•　　　•　　　•　　　•　　　•

It was a quietly jubilant party which gathered on to the after-deck at midnight. None felt like sleep, and those who had been left aboard demanded a full account of the raid. Blake, perforce, had to relate what had happened, and if Yvonne's nearness to him in the shadow impelled him to lengthen the tale somewhat, who can't blame him?

When he had finished he drew out the little bag he had torn from Rymer's neck and handed it to Captain Lamport. Then all hands gathered close while the captain dropped it into his hand and held it up for their inspection.

An involuntary gasp went up at the flaming beauty of it, and in that moment Blake realised exactly how that imprisoned flame would be the symbol of blood during the life of the pearl.

Not the beauty of nature's creation, but the greed of man would make it that.

When Captain Lamport asked him to extend his kindness, and carry the pearl to London to hand over to Lord Cambrey he consented, and once more it returned to his keeping.

It was thought wise to get away at once, so Captain Vaughan went away to give orders to that effect.

Tinker went below to bathe his aching head, and Captain Weeks also decided to depart.

Shortly after Captain and Mrs. Lamport rose and said goodnight, leaving Blake and Yvonne alone. Then the yacht began to get under way, and, by a mutual impulse, they drew their chairs closer in the shadow.

And so they sat and talked in low tones as the slim Fleur-de-Lys stole off through the purple tropical night. What did they say? Ask Blake.

THE END.

[65200 WORDS]

THE END.

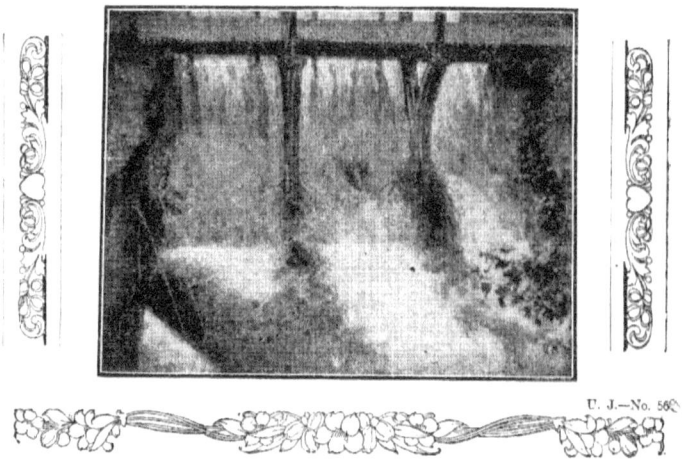

U. J.—No. 56

12,291. CANNIBALS OF SOLOMON ISLANDS. A few real out-and-out specimens with whom one would not trust oneself alone.